# Praise

If the Moon Had Willow Trees | Detroit Eight Series | Book One

*. . . Hall excels at writing natural conversation and witty banter between and among friends and family. Even minor characters seem real and well developed.*

— Five-Star Rating by *Story Circle Book Review*

*. . . prescient of the current political situation . . . the bigotry, segregation and division that remains with us today. It is a coming-of-age story for the author's two main characters, Maggie and Sam, (oh, so in love are they) set against the backdrop of Detroit's racial tension . . . The dialogue rings true. (It is gripping when Loretta, "a Freedom Rider not a Freedom Coaster," takes up the cadence of Dr. King to calm the crowd after his assassination.)*

—Santa Fesina, *Amazon*

*. . . memoir of the past, a companion for current times, and a thought-provoking journey of civil unrest over fifty years . . . While Maggie, Sam and the other uniquely lovable characters are idealistic activists energized for change, on a completely different plane they are intelligent, warm, passionate, ordinary people engaged in intriguing relationships while enjoying the adventure, mystery and passion of their youth.*

—Jo Ann P. McFall, *Amazon*

Livonia | The Whitest City | Detroit Eight Series | Book Two

*. . . a rich tapestry of plots and counter plots woven together during the struggle for civil rights in America . . .*

—Five-Star Rating by *Story Circle Book Review*

*. . . audacity and energy of the cast of characters pulls you in and keeps you company . . . they become your friends. . . . a fast-moving sequel . . . compelling and street-savvy love story . . . the real story is the people—the characters' hopes, dreams and aspirations . . . I'm addicted to this story . . . so well written I need to know what happens next!*

—See reviews on *Amazon and Goodreads*

THE OTHERNESS FACTOR
IPPY Silver Medal for Non-Fiction

*If answered, the writers' call to respect the otherness of those with different world views could go far to help resolve the murderous antagonism that seems to be ripping civilizations apart.*

—Leo McLean, Award-Winning Journalist

*. . . through Socratic discussions . . . an approach to life that promotes self-knowledge, liberation from the ego, and an appreciation and acceptance of diversity.*

—*Kirkus* Review

# ONE WINGBEAT AWAY

A NOVEL

KATHLEEN HALL

ONE WINGBEAT AWAY



A historical fiction, the names and identifying details about named public figures, government entities, places and landmark buildings are based on public records, interviews or the author's personal knowledge. Dates and times of significant historical events are based on public records. Specific quotes by public figures, including artists, musicians, songwriters, gangsters, civil rights' leaders, union leaders, presidents, governors, named mayors and J. Edgar Hoover, are based on public records. However, all dialogue and character descriptions or opinions about events, public figures, organizations, places and landmark buildings, are either products of the author's imagination or are used fictitiously.

Except for public figures, all characters in this book are fictional. Any resemblance to actual people by name, place or occupation is unintentional. In Chapter 21, there's a reference to eleven Canadian soldiers at the *Abbaye d'Ardenne* in Authie, France the day after they were captured at Normandy. This was an actual event; the character involved in the book is fictional. The text reads:

*No doubt he expected the Germans to be on fire with rage after the Normandy landing, but he knew the Geneva Convention protected prisoners of war. On June 7th, the Wehrmacht randomly selected eleven Canadian POWs and marched them to the Abbaye d'Ardenne garden—near the gothic church that served as headquarters for the SS commander.*

The names and ranks of the eleven Canadian POWs who lost their lives that day are honored in the Foreword | The Not Forgotten.

Published by Collaborative Options, LLC, Austin, Texas. Inquiries should be emailed to co.optionstx@gmail.com.



ISBN: eBook: 978-0990390466
ISBN: Paperback: 978-0990390473

Cover Design: Tim Barber, DISSECT DESIGNS
Interior/Print Design: Danielle Acee.authorassistant.com

Typography: Electra, designed by William Addison Dwiggins in 1935, and Futura. designed by Paul Renner in 1927. Either typeface might have been used in this book had it been published in the Seventies

TO THOSE WHO LISTEN FOR WINGBEATS

Also by Kathleen Hall

NONFICTION

*The Otherness Factor: Co-Creating and Sustaining Intentional Relationships*

FICTION

*If the Moon Had Willow Trees*
Detroit Eight Series | Book One

*Livonia | The Whitest City*
Detroit Eight Series | Book Two

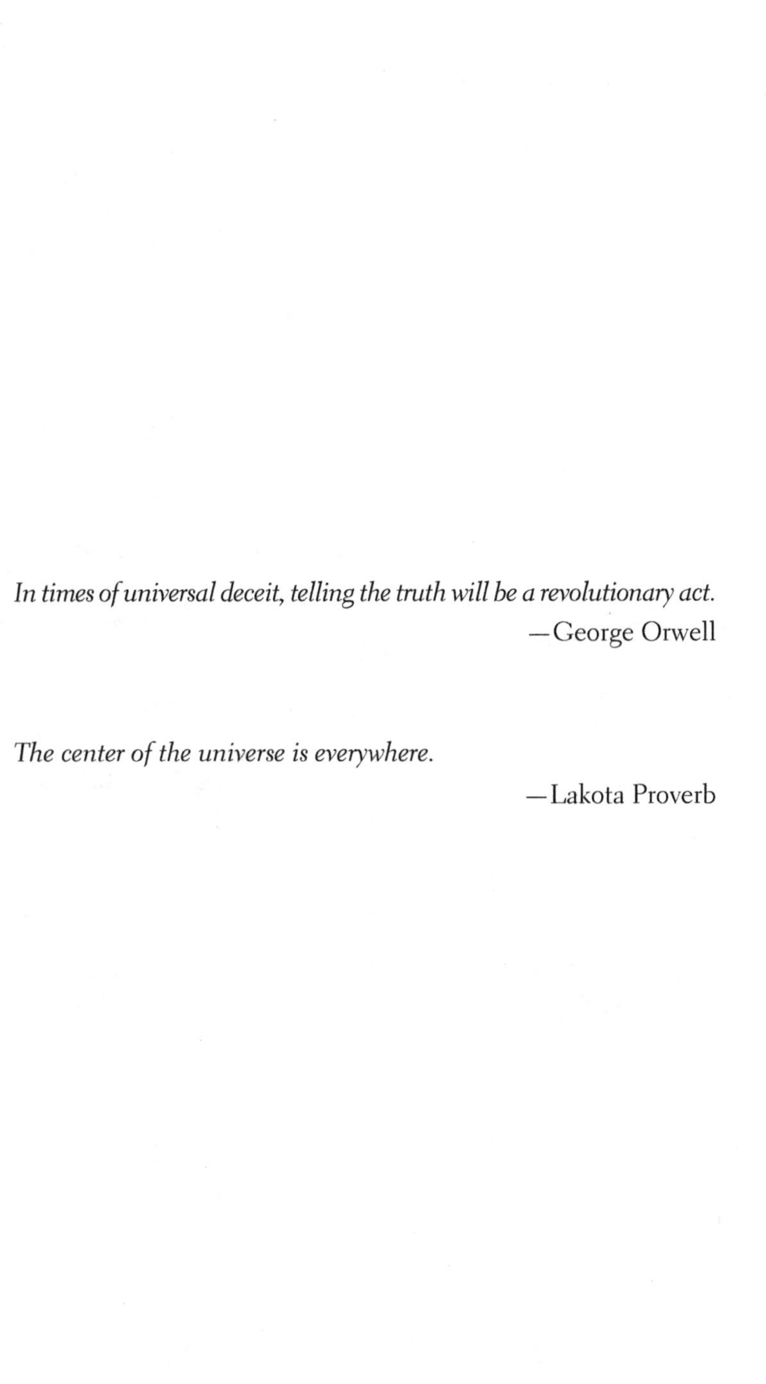

*In times of universal deceit, telling the truth will be a revolutionary act.*

—George Orwell

*The center of the universe is everywhere.*

—Lakota Proverb

# Foreword

## The Not Forgotten

More than one million Canadians joined the Allied Troops to defeat Adolph Hitler's hideous march against civilization in the Second World War. A war that served as a memory, flashback, cause for choices made, risks taken by fictional characters in this book. In my research, I learned the true story of eleven Canadian soldiers who had something to teach me. I am forever changed.

On June 7, 1944, one day after landing on the beaches of Normandy, thousands of Allied soldiers were captured by the Wehrmacht. They must have known, hoped, the Geneva Convention would protect prisoners of war. Yet, at the *Abbaye d'Ardenne,* in Authie, France, eleven Canadian POWs were randomly selected to be executed by the 12$^{th}$ SS Panzer Division, Hitler's Youth. That evening, the soldiers were marched to a garden near a stone church and brutally murdered by boys groomed to be killers.

Far too many died in WWII for a just and moral cause. But the story about these eleven Canadian soldiers found me and taught me about love, dedication, and sacrifice. Until now, I called myself a peacenik. I thought *war* was corrupt and barbaric. I thought the *Nazi's* were crazed outlaws. I thought *intelligence* would rule. I hadn't imagined the stakes.

Today, the world is still on fire with ignorance, racism, and antisemitism. These beautiful Canadians died far too young, too soon, but died for a cause we could not afford to lose. We owe them our freedom. Let's not forget.

North Nova Scotia Highlanders
Private Ivan Crowe
Private Charles Doucette
Corporal Joseph MacIntyre
Private Reginald Keeping
Private James Moss

27th Canadian Armoured Regiment
Trooper James Bolt
Trooper George Gill
Trooper Thomas Henry
Trooper Roger Lockhead
Trooper Harold Philp
Lieutenant Thomas Windsor

# Contents

# From The Author

## Racist Language Advisory

WORDS MATTER. Nouns describing powerless men, women, and children in the US weren't accidental; they were habitual and intentional. For centuries white men ruled, setting the tone and language. History doesn't occur in a vacuum. Conflicts, assassinations, police actions were incited or quelled by leadership intention. Far too often driven by economic interests. Who gained by racial strife, white flight? Whose pockets were lined; whose power was brokered?

WORDS ARE WEAPONS. Most of us want to eradicate hideous words from our language, literature, schools, newspapers, police departments, political arenas. To build a better world, we're finally electing people whose diverse experience, complexion, and perspective represents us.

WORDS DEFINE THE TIMES. During this era, the n-word was common in newspapers, radio programs, national magazines; spoken by governors, mayors, police, scout leaders and teachers. I don't want to incite racism by using the n-word, but there's no way to hide these atrocities under Donna Reed's starched apron. I believe historical novelists have a duty to respect readers and the facts—the times, clothing, food, attitudes, language, influences, events.

WORDS CARRY THE STORY. I take full responsibility for including the godawful n-word and other hateful racist and sexist words when it was historically factual or, in my opinion, essential to the story. A sign on my desk asks: *Does each WORD carry its weight?* Probably not. Yet, I believe history's promise or deceit is better served by different views, voices, stories. This is mine.

# Prologue

ON JANUARY 3, 1969, Sam Tervo had eight files in his briefcase when he walked into the Sheridan-Cadillac Hotel. He'd always thought of this place as the Mafioso Don of downtown hotels—lots of glitz, crystal, and bravado. The message was: do not enter unless you plan to spend serious money, keep your mouth shut, and tip well.

When the hotel opened in 1924, the Book Cadillac, better known as The Book, was Detroit's tallest building and the tallest hotel in the world. With more than one thousand guest rooms, three dining rooms, three ballrooms, it housed the godfather of all lobbies. Downtown dwellers knew The Book was the favorite hang-out for Abe Bernstein and his Purple Gang, Detroit's answer to Al Capone and his Chicago Outfit. In fact, Abe and Al were friends, as far as friends go in crime syndicates. Majordomo Bernstein, who spent his life dodging bullets, imprisonments, and rival gangs, lived on The Book's top floor until he died in 1968 at the age of seventy-six—far surpassing the most generous actuarial tables for gangsters. Many believed Abe haunted The Book, training his eyes on good-looking broads in the lobby, ordaining poker hands in the small salons, and taking a sip of each neat Ballantine's 30-Year Whiskey served at the bar.

Dressed in his gray gabardine suit, white shirt, steel-blue tie, silver and copper cufflinks, Sam thought his new wingtips were overkill. *What perverted, psychopathic urge had possessed him to buy a pair of shoes like his dad's?* With each click of his heel across the marble-tiled lobby, Sam was sure everyone knew he was an imposter, a boy pretending to be a businessman. He had no idea he was catching the setting sun — his high Finnish cheekbones transforming worry into determination, his fiery blue eyes silencing detractors, claiming his power.

That's the thing about big cities and grand hotels, ordinary people get the impression there's a higher power, a pecking order, another world hidden behind these magnificent structures, and they're right.

Eighteen months before Sam walked through that lobby, he was standing behind a wooden barricade in the middle of Fort Street. Wearing an ill-fitting, sweat-drenched National Guard uniform and holding a gun, he watched Detroit burn. It was July 25, 1967, day two of what would become the biggest race-based uprising in American history. For Sam, it was the day Maggie Soulier followed a disc jockey's plea for anyone left in Detroit to deliver drinks to thirsty cops in the middle of nowhere.

That's how things happen in life. Those idiosyncratic choices we make, or don't make, slam us into love, purpose—a future we never planned for, could not possibly imagine.

Maggie would laugh and say she met Sam on the wrong side of his gun. What made this more ridiculous, was Maggie and Sam were anti-war, civil rights activists. They soon uncovered two six-degrees-of-separation connections—both were working-poor grad students at Wayne State, and both called Clyde Webster friend.

Before the rebellion's last ember died, a group of eight civil rights workers sat around Clyde and Blanche Webster's chipped dining-room table and formed The Detroit Eight. Clyde tried to keep a straight face when he introduced Maggie Soulier and Sam Tervo as their token whites. It helped break the ice. Not everyone thought whites deserved attention, much less a seat at the table. In the Sixties, the real work of civil rights happened in kitchens, dining rooms, church basements, and local diners—not in grand hotels. Well, sometimes in grand hotels.

By the Seventies, there were colored stickpins marking major social, economic, and human rights events across the globe. And between these stickpins that whole thing about six-degrees-of-separation began to multiply and spread like a pandemic. Days after Iris Rivera got fired for refusing to make her boss coffee in Chicago, secretaries in Warsaw insisted on their rights.

Sometimes these stickpins find one another and sometimes they're related to one another—like Maggie, the daughter of notorious French-Canadian secessionist radicals Anna and Raymond Soulier. Still wanted by the Canadian Mounties, Anna and Raymond disappeared without a trace along the St. Lawrence Seaway in 1950. Maggie was five, and her sister, Issie, was twelve. During the summer, they lived with Aunt Minnie and Uncle Cyp in Windsor; during the academic year they boarded at the Amadeus School for Girls in Toronto.

Anna and Raymond's benefactor and friend, Jacques Ruivivar, owns Zeno Development in Toronto. His name is on a few of those stickpins. Most notably, Jacques is connected to a well-financed, underground human rights organization called Oz. On the six-degrees calculator, Jacques and Clyde Webster are friends. After Clyde went AWOL during the Vietnam War, Jacques rescued him from the streets and hired his lawyer, Bruce Shelton, to keep Clyde out of jail. According to Clyde, anyone who knows Jacques soon realizes his executive assistant, Catherine Caron, is the person in charge of Zeno. Loretta, Maggie's best friend—one of The Eights and a member of Oz—insists that Catherine also runs Oz.

After Sam and Maggie married, they took a road trip to Toronto in the summer of 1968. Maggie wanted to finally meet 'this Jacques.' For all those growing-up years, he was just a name. For Maggie, he was also her best, maybe last chance, of finding her missing parents. Jacques told Maggie to drop it. She didn't, hasn't, and won't drop it.

# 1

# The Getaway

SATURDAY MORNING, SEPTEMBER 17, 1977—Maggie Tervo loved to remake herself. It wasn't that she didn't like who she was; it was more about the mystical process of tapping into new reserves, trying on new personas. This year was the year of the woman. The National Organization of Women, NOW, would be hosting its first national conference in Houston in November. Now, Maggie decided, was the time to fess up. Instead of remaking herself all these years, she pandered away her life. For eight years she called herself an activist, a feminist, a poet. She was a fraud. *This time,* thought Maggie, *would be different.* Feminism she understood. She lost her job teaching at The University of Detroit because she was pregnant; Penney's refused to give her a credit card until her husband approved; and car dealers treated her like an idiot.

Dropping any pretense of being the dutiful housewife, Maggie unleashed newfound feminist sensibilities—she stopped shaving her legs, wearing a bra, cooking, cleaning, pleasing. Sam Tervo, whose name she took before she discovered feminism, was too captivated by his junior-executive position at Jingo Motors to notice. And undaunted by any isms, Tekla Moonwalker Tervo—who made her inimitable landing at St. Mary's Hospital in Livonia, Michigan the night Neil Armstrong made his leap for mankind on a black and white TV in the delivery room—was lost in that girls-only aging-phenom of being eight-going-on-thirteen.

*Bring on the 'Stepford Wives!'* thought Maggie. We're still saying mankind instead of humankind. And Phyllis Schlafly and her disciples are pursing their lips and preaching seduction, submission, and alimony over freedom. Maggie shook her head and wondered if Mrs. Schlafly ever left her all-white-economically-gifted community.

Since no one was looking, or listening, Maggie made one of those impulsive, electrifying leaps to self-interest. How long had it been since she took off on her own? And why, under any set of circumstances, would leaving for Canada on Saturday instead of Monday seem unreasonable? Why would any adult woman need permission to take a short trip to Canada in a 1962 white Chevy Corvair?

As it turned out, neither Sam nor Tekla seemed interested in her announced change in plans. So why worry about three loads of dirty clothes on the utility room floor, a stack of bills under the grease-stained yellow pages on the kitchen counter, and a near-empty fridge? Maggie took a deep breath and copped a smile as she backed out of the driveway.

Over the past six years, Jacques Ruivivar and Catherine Caron would fly to Detroit to meet them for dinner at the London Chophouse downtown, a picnic on Boblo Island, or a day at Tiger Stadium. Once or twice a year, she, Sam, and Tekla, would cross the Ambassador Bridge to meet them on the Canadian side of the Detroit River to binge on fish and chips at their favorite dive in Windsor. It was during these outings that Maggie began to examine Jacques and Catherine.

Their get-togethers became anthropologic field trips—a chance to look for signs of genetic imprints—skin tones, moles, the arch of an eyebrow, turn of a smile, sound of a laugh. Every outing became a deep dive into DNA. When Maggie got home, she'd record her notes in a black Moleskine notebook reserved for poems, then tuck it under her high school yearbook in the bottom drawer of her *escritoire*. Six years and two Moleskines later, Maggie still couldn't tell, didn't ask, and continued her lifelong habit of imagining, guessing, waiting for the strike of lightning that would illuminate the dark recesses of her mind, memory, and longing to find Anna and Raymond. Maggie shook her head, tightened her grip on the steering wheel, and thought, *screw caution!*

Singing off-key, Maggie began, "I am woman hear me roar." With each verse getting louder, powering her up, Maggie decided to brave the tunnel solo for the first time. Excited and tormented by the idea of being under the Detroit River, Maggie roared, "I am invincible!" —as water seeped through cracks in the darkness and shadows, the smell of exhaust fumes licked her tongue, the fear of being buried alive coaxed each breath—before the shimmer of sunlight pulled her through Customs in Windsor.

The border patrol agent bent down to talk to her through the driver's side window. "Driver's license, please."

Maggie pulled her Michigan license from her wallet and handed it to him.

"Are you Marguerite Tervo?"

"Yes, sir."

"What's your nationality?"

"Canadian."

"Are you a citizen of the United States?"

"No, sir. Not yet."

"Do you have a Canadian driver's license?"

"No, sir."

"Do you reside at the address on your Michigan driver's license?"

"Yes, sir."

"What's your occupation?"

"I'm a . . ."

"I'm sorry, Miss Tervo, but you'll need to speak up. Your occupation?"

"Sorry. I'm a wife and mother. I used to be a teacher."

"What's your purpose for entering Canada?"

"I'm here to visit old friends."

"Where are these friends?"

"In Hamilton and Toronto."

The agent walked behind the car and looked like he was writing down her license plate number.

"How long will you be visiting your friends?"

"I plan to be in Canada for five days."

"Do you have any produce, plants, or animals in your car?"

"No, sir."

He was quiet for a moment, writing something on his pad. Maggie looked at him—late twenties, thick black hair, deep green eyes. He could be a relative.

"What's the name of Canada's national anthem?"

"Sorry, would you repeat your question?"

He had a cheeky smile, pretty teeth. "Of course, my question is, do you know the name of Canada's *unofficial* national anthem?"

Maggie nodded and said, "'O Canada.'"

"Canada's national symbol?"

"Maple leaf!" Maggie felt as if she was in her third-grade geography class, thrilled to know the right answer.

"What's your favorite hockey team?"

Maggie looked into the agent's eyes; he was playing with her, maybe flirting. She said, "That's a push. A few years ago, I would have said the Maple Leafs, but now it's the Red Wings."

He shook his head, whistled air through clenched teeth, and said, "This is not good. I hope you'll reconsider your answer while you're here." He then patted the door under her open window, bent his head down, and said, "Pay attention to speed-limit signs, Marguerite Tervo, and enjoy your time back home."

Maggie felt a childlike exuberance when she exclaimed, "I will!" As she moved past the checkpoint area, she looked in the rear-view mirror. The reflection of her eyes delighted her imagination. Who was this woman driving to Canada on her own, free of husband, daughter, household obligations? She breathed in the crisp, chill air. September signaled new beginnings—freshly-sharpened yellow pencils; an unmarked three-ring blue canvas notebook; and clean, blue-lined sheets of paper—as she waited for the bell to ring.

# 2

# Pay Dirt

MONDAY EVENING, SEPTEMBER 19, 1977—Before dark, Maggie had trekked through dozens of milled-tree pages, and hundreds of microfilm files, in musty public record offices and some of the most modern, well-stocked, eclectic libraries she'd ever seen. No one asked for her birth certificate or driver's license—just her signature and ten-cents-per-page for copies.

At each stop, she found court documents or microfilmed newspaper articles about the disappearance and criminal charges against her parents, Anna and Raymond Soulier. Some included photographs that Maggie studied until she lost track of time and place. When Anna and Raymond disappeared in 1950, they were on Jacques Ruivivar's boat along the St. Lawrence Seaway. There were no bodies, no trace evidence, nothing. Jacques, her parent's closest friend and patron, was named conservator of funds set aside for her and her sister Issie.

Records and articles about Jacques, his company Zeno Development, and her and Issie's boarding school, Amadeus School for Girls, were more random, idiosyncratic, and mundane. When Catherine showed up in a photo from a recent Amadeus School fundraiser, Maggie compared her photo to earlier photos of Anna and convinced herself they were the same person. Then, shaking her head, she edited her observations to decide, no, definitely not!

Aunt Jo, her mother's younger sister, showed up in a microfilmed 1937 *Windsor Star* news clip: "Josephine Landry Wins Province-Wide High School Tennis Tournament." Aunt Jo's lover, Phillip Xavier, killed in World War II, brought up a simple obituary—a short bio about being raised in Hamilton and graduating from Assumption College in Windsor, before joining the Royal Canadian Army. But Maggie hit pay-dirt when she looked for information about *La Bière*—a Canadian brewing company that ranked high on Oz's watch list and had haunted Sam since his night shifts at Sheer Juice.

For decades *La Bière* had partnered with or acquired juice companies interested in using a preservative to prolong the shelf-life of fresh juices. Initially targeted for mixed drinks in bars, this same preservative had gained wide-spread popularity for most fruit beverages and some beers. According to Sam, Clyde, and Jacques, *La Bière* had been, and might still be, involved in a scheme to make and sell adulterated fruit drinks as 'one-hundred percent pure juice.' Based on Oz's research, the preservative is deadly. Since the cost of producing the adulterated juice was radically less expensive than bottling pure juice and buying it back when it expired, the preservative meant hundreds of millions, if not billions, in profits for juice bottlers—or beer companies who hitched onto this ominous star.

Mostly sugar and preservative, the adulterated juices contained scant quantities of natural juice and pulp. The preservative—shipped in blue plastic containers marked DEPC for diethyl polycarbonate—had been banned in the States since 1972, after Swedish scientists discovered DEPC reacted with the juice to form urethane, a known carcinogen. There was no ban on DEPC as an industrial cleaner. Shipped into Canada and across the border into the U.S., the 'industrial cleaner' arrived at juice companies in unmarked panel trucks. Maggie shuddered at the thought of babies drinking poisoned juice through rubber nipples on colorful Evenflo plastic bottles, toddlers sipping from their first Tupperware tumblers, teens quenching their thirst at open refrigerator doors.

When *La Bière* promotes and sells poison-laced juice for profit, the decisions are made by men in three-piece suits in corporate offices. Executives with gold cufflinks and manicured nails who hire 'mules' to transport the 'industrial cleaner' across the border while they attend their daughter's recital at a private school. No one looks menacing, and no one blows the whistle. While Maggie was combing public records and news reports, she planned to strip *La Bière* down to the marrow of all records, including past and pending lawsuits. After years of talking-the-walk and calling herself an activist, Maggie was desperate to act—to put herself out-there, wherever out-there was.

Evening blended into the deserted beige-on-beige standard-fare hotel lobby when Maggie walked in with a large brown grocery sack filled with documents. Almost six-thirty, Maggie was sure she'd fall asleep without eating if she headed to her room. Maybe a glass of wine and a sandwich while she read through the Xerox copies and came up with questions to ask Catherine. Or not. Maggie realized she'd been so busy moving from point A to point B that she was missing the experience of being alone on this trip.

The dimly lit, funky hotel bar was empty. She put the sack down at her feet, pulled herself up on a heavy, black vinyl barstool, hung her purse from a hook under the bar, then ran her hand across the polished mahogany lip at the edge of the counter.

"Fewer spills," said the barkeep, a middle-aged man with thinning salt-and-pepper hair, broken blood vessels under pale skin, and what Aunt Jo would call a toothsome smile. Not perfect teeth, but well-lived teeth. Teeth that enjoyed a proper brushing, but showed signs of age—yellow, cement-patched, likely tin-amalgam-filled teeth—twisting sideways to find space. As Maggie reached into her purse for her Moleskine to record her observations, reality struck. She was the woman sitting on a barstool by herself in Canada.

"Miss? Are you all right?"

Maggie looked into the barkeep's hooded blue eyes for an uncomfortable moment before she laughed and said, "Sorry. It's been a long day, and my mind was chasing a few fugitive thoughts."

"Wild desperados, all of 'em! Every day I lose more thoughts than I catch," he grinned. "Name's Steve. I'm the bartender, waiter, and cook. Can I get you a drink, menu, or both?"

"Name's Maggie. How about a Beaujolais and your favorite menu item unless it's oysters or snails; nothing that slides across the plate."

"Fish and chips, it is. Based on your French accent, catsup instead of vinegar for the fries?"

"Good guess. Not that I have anything against vinegar," Maggie laughed.

Steve filled a small flute with red wine. "Born and raised in upstate New York and crossed the St. Lawrence to avoid the draft; never found a reason to move back. I'm one of those accidental Canadians. Can't claim the French, Brits or Americans."

"Vietnam?"

"Yep. I know. I look old enough to be a Korean-era vet, but it was a Vietnam dodge. A year after I got here, leukemia knocked me on my ass. Lost my youth, my ability to procreate, but not my soul." Steve tapped the counter as he walked away, like the border patrol agent who patted the side of her car.

Like Bruce Shelton the day she attended her first Oz meeting in 1971 when he slapped his hand on the table and said, "No meltdowns. None. Bite your tongue if you have to, but do not fall apart." Maggie realized she'd been biting her tongue for six years as they all pretended to be normal—subjugating her power to an organization she hadn't yet joined or declined.

Tekla was her sun and moon; Sam, at best an unreliable keeper of vows and promises, at worst a serial womanizer. And her bizarre attraction to Bruce? A still-life memory of walking across floes of ice in search of warmth. Maggie took a sip of wine, closed her eyes, and felt the nectar tug at her throat.

# 3

## Six Years Ago
# The Cutting Room Floor

OCTOBER 1971—Weeks after her first Oz meeting in September, Maggie couldn't get Bruce off her mind. Over and over, she thought, *who the hell does he think he is?* No one had ever threatened her, talked to her like she was a sleaze. *What an asshole!* Like an abused wife, Maggie kept it secret. She was too embarrassed to tell anyone—not Sam, Issie, nor any of her friends. No one.

Then, on a warm orange-leaved day in late October, Maggie called Issie to see if she'd watch Tekla for a few hours so she could recalibrate—check out a few libraries and stop by the cider mill without a tired, ornery two-year-old. Issie didn't need a reason, and Tekla loved roughhousing with the boys.

When Maggie pulled up to Issie and Eddie's brick and asphalt ranch—an aging GI Loan tract house in Westland—two Whiffle balls; two croquet mallets; and an unlaced, child-sized baseball mitt littered the front yard. Issie was sitting on the porch next to a UAW coffee mug holding down a want-ad section from the *Detroit Free Press*.

"Hey, Iss, Tekla's ready for game day at the Austin's!"

Issie jumped off the porch with a growl, squatted like a catcher on the sidewalk, spread her arms, and called, "Come here, you little stinkpot, and give your favorite Aunt Issie a big hug!"

Tekla ran full force into Issie's arms, knocked her down and cried, "NO STINKPOT! PUMPKIN GIRL!"

Lifting Tekla in the air, Issie gave her a long, bug-eyed look before saying, "Oh, my. How did I get that wrong? You are the one and only Pumpkin Girl who talks in capital letters and exclamation points. Now I remember."

Maggie glanced at the want-ad section and decided the conversation about Issie's job search could wait. Eddie's latest innovation—Egg On The Run, a mobile diner for blue-collar worksites—meant major bucks: a tricked-out travel trailer, advertising, food-service licenses, insurance, you name it. Issie had been CEO, driver, accountant, publicist, cook, on-the-job mechanic. Her wicked determination, sixteen-hour days, and two-dollar meals couldn't keep pace with the cost of operations. She and Eddie had to get a loan to pay off the bills and sell the trailer and equipment at a loss.

Shaking off some residual guilt, Maggie headed to her car with a backward wave before Issie offered coffee, before she lost her nerve—which raised the question of how we hold on to nerve. Maggie knew she was about to find out. After nailing down the time with Issie earlier that morning, Maggie called Bruce.

"Bruce Shelton's office, may I help you?"

"Hey, Carol, Maggie Tervo. How are you?"

"Fine, Maggie. How are you? I thought we were going to judo together by now."

"Oh, god. My plans and schemes always seem to end up on the cutting room floor."

"Kahlil Gibran. *The Prophet*?"

"I think it's *The Prophet*. Maybe not. My mind is turning to mush. The risk of hanging out with a toddler."

"How's Miss Moonwalker?"

Maggie laughed, "Tekla's either on-strike or protesting some imagined slight. My new theory is activists were suppressed as two-year-olds."

"You?"

"Yes, me. Plus, Sam, Loretta, Clyde, Blanche; most of The Detroit Eights. We were all shushed and told not to complain, make a fuss, or draw attention to ourselves. I'm surprised there aren't more of us. You?"

"No way. My Italian family shouted, cried, threw spaghetti—part of our DNA. Other than a few Catholic doctrines I blew off like dry dandelions, and a crazy mobster uncle who went nutso when we kids got too loud, I don't remember being shushed."

"Hmm . . . glad to know it works. I get the looks and comments when Tekla pitches a fit or has a sit-down strike in public. Such a fine line between expressing our self and offending unintended listeners. Like you. Am I talking too much?"

"You're kidding, right? I'm stuck with criminals, judges, and attorneys—a bunch of gorillas who act like they're part of some hunt and grunt club. Believe me; it's nice to talk to another sentient being. I assume you want Bruce. Let me see where he is."

After a slight pause, Bruce picked up and whispered, "Mis...sus Ter...vo, what brings you to the dark side?"

"Out slumming and thought I'd give you a call. Any chance you're free for lunch?"

Maggie felt the smile on Bruce's face when he said, "I'm up for slumming, but no can do. If you want to grab lunch here, come by at noon. I'll have Carol pick something up at the deli. I've got to leave at one for a hearing, which gives us an hour. Work for you?"

"Sure."

Bruce whispered, "So, little sister, any agenda? What can I do to prepare?"

Maggie's knees began to bounce up and down; she was under no illusions. Indignation didn't cause her blush, racing heart, or swollen clit. Although Maggie shook her head as if she was telling herself no, she couldn't pretend her planned confrontation with Bruce was based on high moral ground—pretend this wasn't her response to signals she felt the night Bruce slammed his hand on her desk and whispered in her ear. If Bruce treated her like a skank, and she felt aroused, did that make her a skank? Or did it simply mean she was human—longing for a quick fix to fill the void, a band-aid for the soul? Whatever it was, Maggie knew the door to the cutting room floor was still wide open. She could end it here, right now, with no questions, no temptation, no rodeo ride.

"Mr. Shelton, if I didn't know better, I'd say you were on the make. Just lunch and some free legal advice."

Bruce was in a full-throttled laugh when he said, "Game on, Mrs. Tervo. If Carol isn't up front, head to my office at the end of the hall."

High noon, that shadow-less space on the Gregorian clock, seemed stacked with undelivered omens when Maggie pulled up to Bruce's office. She had no doubt the next sixty minutes would shake the narrow expanse of Oz's metaphorical rope bridge. The bridge she found herself on last March after being hijacked by Sam, Clyde, Bruce, and Jacques in the wine cellar at the Marcus Red Fox Restaurant—an encounter Maggie called her 'shock treatment.' Oz might demand loyalty to make global changes, but she was not for sale.

'Bruce Shelton, Attorney-At-Law' was painted across a long, narrow sign over a black wrought-iron, twelve-pane French door. Inside the remodeled post-office—antique-brass postal boxes, two old church pews and a well-worn oak counter in the reception area lit by simple glass globes. Carol wasn't up front.

To the right of the reception counter, a steel and wired-glass industrial door looked more imposing than inviting. Maggie hesitated.

"Door's open, Mrs. Tervo. Lunch is ready," Bruce's disembodied voice boomed over a PA speaker behind her, above the outside door. Maggie looked around to see if there was a camera.

With an exaggerated stage whisper, Bruce said, "Maggie, you won't find a camera. Besides, you're the only person I'm expecting at noon."

Maggie shook her shoulders, arms, and hands and took a deep breath before she pulled the door open. The four-foot-wide hallway was spare—no tables, umbrella racks, or coat hooks. On the wall to her right, three abstract paintings; on the wall to her left, a swinging gate to the reception area and three closed doors.

At the end of the hall, Bruce was leaning against the door jamb, grinning like a nine-year-old at Edgewater Park. "I said you wouldn't find a camera; I didn't say there wasn't a camera. What are you so hyped up about?"

Maggie felt the color rise in her cheeks before her fight-or-flight response grabbed her solar plexus and iced her resolve. "We need to talk. We can do it over lunch or another time."

"By all means, little sister. We've got Greek salad and gyros. Come on in."

Bruce's office looked like it was lifted from his house. Hand-rubbed white painted walls, indirect lighting, custom-made white maple cabinets, and a long, curved white maple desk with three matching visitor chairs in the Eero Saarinen mid-century-modern look.

"Nice! Your desk reminds me of the lobby desk at Zeno Development, Jacques' building in Toronto."

"My second home. When it comes to design, I'm a shameless plagiarist. After Eames, Saarinen, and Jacobsen, what's left?"

Two lunches—across the desk from one another—sat on bamboo placemats with gray linen napkins, stainless flatware, and a pot of coffee with two white mugs in easy reach.

"Let's eat. I'm all yours for the next hour."

Maggie looked at Bruce—narrow-cut black gabardine slacks, a black crewneck over a white button-down shirt, sleeves pushed up, his gray hair pulled into a short ponytail. At thirty-six, people might tag him an aging hippie, but Maggie knew he was an outlier, an edge walker. His pock-marked face and gaunt, angular body conveyed the pain of rejection, outsider status, mortal loneliness.

"Thanks. It might not take an hour. Although I'd like to keep this between us, I know we're bit players on a large stage. I won't ask you to keep this to yourself."

Bruce placed his fork on his plate and leaned back. "Huh? For some reason, I was suffering under the delusion this was going to be more personal, perhaps sensual. You surprise me, Mrs. Tervo."

"I doubt that, Mr. Shelton. My guess is you see yourself as the maestro—out of the fray but invested in the outcome, willing to test the ice but not risk exposure."

Bruce picked up his fork and stabbed a small piece of cucumber, a tomato wedge, a strip of red onion, and took his first bite.

"It appears I underestimated you, little sister. Go on."

"Even now, you're playing with me. You may think I'm some insipid housewife wasting away in Livonia, but I'm here to tell you I'm my own person and . . ."

"What the hell does it mean to be your own person? You're kidding, right?"

Maggie shook her head, "Wrong. I'm not kidding you. Your charm, wealth, status, and intimidating reputation in the courtroom serves you well. Those tools might influence others, but not me."

"And what, Mrs. Tervo, influences you?"

"Knowledge. I want to know why Oz tapped Clyde, Blanche, Loretta, Sam and me, but not Stella, Willie and Robin—the other Eights."

"Maggie, Oz doesn't invite groups to join, they vet individuals. You tell me. Why wouldn't Oz recruit Stella, Willie and Robin?"

"I have no idea."

"Dumb doesn't work. Think. What common personality traits do these three remarkable people have that makes them poor choices for Oz?"

Maggie's competitive spirit grabbed hold as she thought about characteristics that separated these three from the rest of The Eights. *Okay*, she thought, *Willie has a short fuse and can get combative; but his work to keep blacks out of jail takes rigorous patience and tact. His wife Robin—Detroit's famous cakemaker—is precise and particular; she refuses to bake more than a certain number of cakes per month. Period, no wiggle room. If Aretha Franklin called, she'd turn her down. Robin is without doubt, the most focused and least flexible. Then there's Stella, filled with hope and energy; her kindness and guilelessness make her an easy target. Her willingness to accommodate everyone comes off as needy but takes great energy and courage. Like hooking up with Kenny, Sam's brother, a white man.*

"I'm batting zero."

"Think. Weaknesses are almost always over-extended strengths. I want you to step up to the plate and try again."

Maggie closed her eyes and flipped through the characteristics of all three and realized each had rigid systems in place to mimic control. With Willie, it was the constant tension between combativeness and patience. For Robin it was the rigor of inflexibility. For Stella, it was the crushing burden of over-pleasing. Maggie nodded her head, looked at Bruce and said, "How about rigidity, control and predictability?"

"I'd say that covers it. The Eights who made the cut have enough confidence and creativity to find new routes, new ways of accomplishing their work. That doesn't mean they're smarter, it means their temperaments are better suited to the unknown, untested. It's easy to teach new skills, but near impossible to change someone's attitude or temperament."

"What if The Eights who made the cut are needier? Like me. Maybe we need a group to prop us up."

"Maggie, don't jack with this. People get pushed off the proverbial rope bridge every week. There's no room for mavericks. Not me, not you, not anyone. Capisce?"

"No, I don't get it, and I don't agree. I want you to hear me say I'm not for sale, I'm not joining a cult, and I sure as hell am not going to follow you across that rickety bridge."

"Cut. Take. You're not for sale. What's your next scene, Maggie?"

"There's no next scene. I want answers. What is Oz? Who are their friends, enemies, comrades in arms? What have they done to make this a better world?"

"Here's the rub. I want you to listen to me. By the time you come up with the right questions, you'll know the answers. Knowledge is not knowing; knowing is knowledge. Knowing takes work, lifetimes. Being part of Oz is not for people who think they've arrived because they finished some Dewey Decimal System marathon or passed the Bar."

Maggie's early-warning-leg was bouncing up and down again. Her cool, icy reserve a puddle threatening to spill down her cheeks. Bruce looked at Maggie and waited for her next volley.

Leaning forward, Maggie edged up on her chair, hiked her purse strap over her shoulder, and looked toward the door. Then, without another word, she stood up, walked around the desk, and reached for Bruce's hand. He held her eyes as he pulled her onto his lap, wrapped his arms around her, and began slowly rocking his Arne Jacobsen Egg Chair. *Like a nest,* thought Maggie.

# 4

# Tempus Fugit

MONDAY EVENING, SEPTEMBER 19, 1977—"*Tempus fugit,*" said Maggie, as she pulled her fringed, black-suede purse off the hook and settled her tab with Steve. She couldn't remember the last time she had to calculate a tip. What was it now, fifteen percent? Maggie placed twelve Canadian dollars on the ten-dollar tab. She'd waited enough tables to know the extra fifty-cent tip was a meager but appreciated bump.

"Time does fly," said Steve. "How long are you here?"

"A few days. Then . . . I lean on my friends," laughed Maggie as she slid off the barstool.

The sluggish elevator caused Maggie second and third thoughts. From now on, she'd take the stairs. Although her room was bare-bones, with one double bed and a small desk with a chair—the mattress was firm, and the sheets and pillowcases were fresh. Exhausted by her long day, Maggie stretched out on the white Matelassé spread and let her shoes drop to the floor. Fighting an impulse to turn on her side and close her eyes, Maggie bounded out of bed, stripped her clothes off, then turned the shower on before she realized she'd left her paper bag under the bar. *Damn!* She threw her soiled clothes back on, slid into her shoes, and ran down the steps.

Two men were sitting at the bar; a kerchiefed woman was the lone diner in an alcove of small tables near the back. *Steve must be in the kitchen,* thought Maggie, as she walked up to the two men and said, "Excuse me. Did either of you see a bag under the bar when you sat down?"

"I've never heard that line before," laughed the older of the two men. Balding with a desperate comb-over of auburn strands, he was wearing a hunter-green wool sport coat with a name tag that read: Bob McDougal—Member in Good Standing—Ontario Hot Mix Producers Association. When Bob saw Maggie reading his nametag, he tapped his badge and said, "I know, hot mix sounds raunchy, but it means asphalt. We're road builders, not porn stars," causing Bob's chum to throw his head back in laughter and choke on his drink.

"Mr. McDougal, I'm sure you and your friend are having a prodigious time. My only question is whether or not you found a brown paper bag under the bar when you walked in."

"No, sir, ma'am! We do not do pro-diggy-ous, but it might be fun," Bob slurred as he saluted Maggie and gave his chum a wink.

"Hey, Maggie," called Steve. He waved her over and whispered, "Are those bad boys giving you a rough time?"

Maggie rolled her eyes and said, "Totally blitzed. No doubt they think they're charming. After I got to my room, I realized I left a bag filled with research documents at the foot of the barstool. I'm hoping you found it and put it in a safe place."

Steve shook his head. "Sorry, Maggie. After you left, the bar was empty. I propped the side door open to get some air and have a smoke. Didn't hear a thing until those two numb nuts walked in. Maybe you left it in your car. You were chasing thoughts when you first got here, eh?"

"I remember putting the bag at my feet so I wouldn't forget. Ha! Great plan that turned out to be. I'll check the front desk."

Before Maggie walked out of the bar, Bob McDougal caught her eye, and the look he gave her was piercing and stone sober. She felt the creep of goose pimples on her arms and legs. It took all her focus to remain upright, walk to the lobby desk, and ask the clerk if he'd seen anyone with a paper bag.

"Sorry, Mrs. Tervo. You're the only guest I saw carrying a grocery sack."

This time, Maggie took the stairs whispering, "He said with disdain dripping from each consonant." Who would care about a paper bag filled with random Xerox copies? Does *La Bière* offer civil service clerks a box seat at a Toronto Maple Leafs' game in exchange for a heads-up when someone scours their corporate records? Or Oz? They must have enough sway to track U.S.-Canadian border crossings of friends and enemies. Or maybe her plan to travel solo to Canada set off alarms for Jacques.

For the past six years, Sam, Clyde, Blanche, Loretta and Aunt Jo had morphed into a rogues' gallery of clucking tongues, reminding Maggie she had no idea who she was dealing with—bad guys who either killed or kidnapped her parents, who wanted to hurt her, her family. Maggie's first crazed impulse was to run up to the rooftop and yell, "COME AND GET ME!" Instead, she dropped to her knees in front of her door and listened. No sounds. The light she'd left on was glancing across the thin threshold. Maggie stood, put her key in the lock, before someone yanked the door open from the inside, and pulled her in.

The paper bag was tipped over on the floor; her copies spilled across the small desk. Bruce filled the narrow entryway and seemed to look through her. *Like the biblical jackal that stands for loneliness, isolation, abandonment,* thought Maggie—*Bruce's 'life thesis' to avoid emotional distractions in his quest to save the world.*

"Sit," said Bruce as he turned and pointed to the end of the bed.

Before Maggie had a chance to think about bolting, Bruce put his arms around her, pulled her close, and whispered, "No, you don't. We're going to sit and talk until you get this right."

Maggie pulled her right arm back to grab the doorknob at the same moment Bruce picked her up and moved her to the end of the bed and forced her to sit.

"No more games, Maggie. There are two men with me—one outside the door and another in the lobby. You're not going to break loose until we've talked; until I say so. *Capisce?*" Bruce pulled the small desk chair out, sat on it backward—his elbows propped on the chair's back—like some noir detective in a B-grade movie. Maggie wanted to laugh.

Instead, she looked at Bruce without a tilt of her head or hint in her eye. Maggie wondered what kind of perverted, crooked force had triggered her romantic interest in him. Of all the men she'd known, and the few she'd dated and slept with, Bruce was the least likely to offer warmth, comfort, attention, or fidelity. He embodied the untouchable, remote, un-love Maggie chased until Sam showed up wagging good-natured kindness and generosity. She and Sam had somehow found their groove in the messy kind of love unearthed by marriage—threatened by impatience, disappointment, fear, and the irresistible push-pull of dependence and independence. Add to that, Sam's two mysterious encounters with the underworld and naked women, Maggie knew a perfect mate was delusional, yet she was the one who seduced Bruce in the Egg Chair. *Holy mother of god, am I still trolling for the strong, silent, unreachable father figure—or doomed by some constant, unmet need for abandonment?*

"Talk to me, Maggie. What's going on?"

"How did you know I was here? Jacques?"

"I'll ask the questions, you answer. You can start by telling me why you're here."

Maggie looked around the room to stall while she considered her answer. She had every right to be here. Anna and Raymond were her parents. *La Bière* might be another matter, but not her parents. "For starters, I'm here because it's been six years since I found out about Oz, and I still don't know if my parents are dead or alive. Is Catherine my mother hiding under plastic surgery and a new identity? Is Jacques, or Raymond, my father? Questions I have a right to ask."

"Maggie, we've been through this before, many times. It doesn't fucking matter. What matters is Oz. What matters is free speech, free will—the health of our planet and the people who call it home.

"Got it. Right now, I'm expressing my free will to find my parents and solve this mystery once and for all. I need closure."

Bruce stared at Maggie as if he could hear her thoughts, read her mind, realign her scattered conundrums like Lincoln Logs. He said nothing.

"What about my free will?"

"You tell me, little sister. Does free will mean we ignore the rights of others? Invite greed and mayhem? Is it okay to divert a stream that provides scarce water to millions of poor, urban tenement dwellers, because a few influential investors want to make a killing on a golf course in the Mojave Desert? At the farthest extremes, what about anarchists who kill millions of people who don't share their world view? Tell me, are you so lost in the story you began at age five that you can't see the risk to yourself, Sam, Tekla, Jacques, Catherine, me—not to mention the decades of work by Oz? Think about it. If Jacques or Catherine know the answers to your questions, why haven't they told you? How far have you stretched your imagination to conclude it must be some simple oversight? Wake up, Mrs. Tervo. You're sleepwalking."

Just a few minutes ago, Maggie wanted to curl up in that oh-so-sweet niche of martyrdom and recount every misfortune, failure, disappointment. But now, as if Bruce had handed her a slide carousel, Maggie began to click through her crafted story. Had she been lost in an historical fiction, a forged memoir, someone else's tragedy? In real life, she'd learned—over and over again—there are no hard-stop beginnings and endings, no closures, just the moment-to-moment of the extraordinary in-between.

"Tell me why you responded to my flirtations?" asked Maggie.

"You mean sexual advances?"

"Okay, sexual advances."

Bruce nodded and said, "I'll answer that. I wanted to see how far you'd go. It was a test."

"What kind of test?"

"I was preparing to walk away, but you walked first."

Whispering, Maggie said, "And what, Barrister Shelton, did that tell you?"

"It told me you wouldn't divert the stream."

Maggie heard someone knock on a nearby door and call, "Room Service." At almost nine o'clock, Sam and Tekla would be waiting for her call.

"You're right. I've been sleepwalking. I spent most of my life trying to rescue my parents and force some happily-ever-after ending."

"How would you know?" asked Bruce.

"Know what?"

"Whether the end would be happy." Bruce smiled, and Maggie delighted in his face lighting up, softening. Once—when she tried to take on Bruce's grimness and improve his happiness quotient—he told her hijacking someone's self-determination was a mortal sin, a capital offense. Maggie looked away and shook her head, thinking how warped it was to believe she, of all people, was qualified to rewrite someone else's life, make them happy—whatever the hell that meant.

As if he read her thoughts, Bruce said, "Maggie, we've all carried those dog-eared manuscripts around in our attempt to edit reality. It's hard to let go. Tomorrow we'll go through these papers and piece together conversations you had with librarians, clerks, anyone. Stay put until you hear from me in the morning."

"The hot mix paver in the green sports coat? He with you?"

"He's with us, Maggie. If you call out, he'll be here in a flash."

"Why would I call out?"

"*La Bière's* connected and there's an outrageous amount of money and power at risk. You set off some alarms. They'll want to learn as much as they can about you. After I leave, call Sam, and keep it cheery, family-like. Assume someone's listening."

"You?"

"No, Maggie, not me."

# 5

# Cat's in the Cradle

MONDAY EVENING, SEPTEMBER 19, 1977—When Harry Chapin's "Cat's in the Cradle" hit the charts in 1972, Maggie was twenty-seven and remembered identifying with the neglected son, not the parent, lip-syncing, . . . *when you coming home, Dad? I don't know when, but we'll get together then. You know we'll have a good time then.*

At thirty-two, with an eight-year-old daughter, Maggie knew she was uncooked, an adolescent crying for attention—scribbling notes in her Moleskine, attempting poetry, trailing The Eights as if she had a single clue about fighting racism, and seducing her husband's friend and lawyer. For years, her long-publicized plan was to return to teaching when Tekla started school. That was three years ago; nothing happened. At the time, Maggie felt stung that no one seemed to care when another one of her plans had crashed and burned, least of all her.

"Hey, Moonwalker, what's up?"

"Ugh. You always say, 'what's up?' There's nothing up."

"Okay, what's down?"

"Corny with a capital C. Sam, Maggie's on the phone!"

"Tekla, wait! I want to talk."

"Hey, Mag, we're missing you back here in this wild and crazy burb."

"Not everyone. Tekla just flew off the phone. What's going on?"

"No idea. Ma took her out for pizza tonight; they both had new jokes to try out on me," laughed Sam.

"Like what?"

"Knock-knock jokes that made no sense at all but sent them into manic giggles."

"Gimme your best shot."

"Hmm. Knock-knock,"

"Who's there?"

"Room Service," someone called from outside Maggie's door.

"Whoops—hold on! Room Service has the wrong room."

"Hello! Hey, Mag? Did you forget me on the phone? You there?" Sam heard a click, then nothing. "Hey, Mag, are you there? I'll call back."

Sam's scribbled notes about Maggie's trip were on the back of a Detroit Edison envelope. After rummaging through the junk drawer in the kitchen and emptying the wastebasket, he remembered tucking it in one of the cubby holes in his dad's old secretary, now Maggie's *escritoire*.

"Good evening, Royal Connaught Hotel. May I help you?"

"Yes, please. I was just talking to my wife, Maggie, Marguerite Tervo, and we were disconnected."

"Let me check. No, sorry. We don't have anyone by that name."

"I'm sure she's there. Try Marguerite Soulier, S – O – U . . ."

"Yes, sir. I'm familiar with the name Soulier. We have no one by the name Tervo or Soulier."

"Is there another hotel in Hamilton with a name that sounds like Royal Connaught?"

"No, sir. We're the only hotel by this name. Is there anything else I can do to assist you?"

"Yes. Will you please check again? I just talked to her—I'm sure she's there."

"I appreciate your concern, Mr. Tervo, but no one named Marguerite, Tervo or Soulier, is registered at our hotel. Is there anything else?"

Sam wanted to rip this guy a new one, but he was painfully aware of his growing tendency to tune out Maggie when she was talking. Had he missed her change of plans? "Yes, please. If Marguerite shows up, will you ask her to call home?"

"Of course. I'll also make a note of it for the next shift."

Like the constant rewinding of a faded clip from a home movie, Maggie sorted through her cloudy memory—trying to restore the sights, sounds, shock, and struggle, before someone held a cloth over her nose and mouth. The smell of chemicals made Maggie feel ethereal, groundless. People were talking in the front seat, but she couldn't pick out the words. Jarred by the constant shifting of gears, sharp turn after sharp turn, Maggie wanted to cry "slow down," but nothing worked. Before she put the words together, Maggie forgot what she was going to say. When she tried to sit up to tap the driver's shoulder, the effort seemed too complex. From the front seat, a woman whispered in French, "*Ça va, Marguerite. Dors maintenant, dors,*" then repeated in English, "You're okay, Marguerite. Sleep now, sleep." Maggie closed her eyes.

Clyde picked up on the third ring.

"Hey, Clyde, I need your close attention. You free to talk?"

"Your lucky day, Sam. You caught me before my other slipper hit the floor. No kidding, I'm wearing old-man slippers. What's going on?"

Sam took a deep breath; Clyde's response meant they were on a secure line.

"The Clockwork Orange is ticking. I just talked to Maggie—she's in Hamilton, as in Canada. The ruse was she wanted to connect with old friends, experience the world on her own; no doubt, another attempt to find her parents. Before she left, she called Jacques. He told her he'd be on the road, but Catherine would be in Toronto. Tonight, while we were talking, someone knocked on her door and called 'Room Service.' Maggie put the phone down to tell them they had the wrong room. I heard some noise, then nothing. The phone clicked off. I called the Royal Connaught Hotel, where Maggie planned to stay. The front desk clerk said Maggie was never there. Claims no one with the name Tervo or Soulier had checked in. I think they've got her."

"Let's move with Orange. You and Tekla only—no clothes, no books, nothing. You've got forty minutes before we meet at the dead end."

# 6

# The Grand Prix

MONDAY NIGHT-TUESDAY MORNING, SEPTEMBER 19-20, 1977—Maggie's skull felt tippy and heavy, like one of those enormous papier-mâché heads in a Mardi Gras parade. The race to get wherever they were going must have ended. Now she felt the vibration of an engine and the sound of propellers. When she attempted to open her eyes, something was in the way. A scarf? Maggie wanted to lift the fabric, but her hands were tied to the arms of her seat. When she tried to speak, she felt the same cloth over her mouth. Her panic was hot, immediate, and paralyzing. She wanted to call 'help,' but her throat was too raw to form the word. Resting her head against the inside of the aircraft, she listened to the engine drone. It sounded like a plane, a small plane, maybe a helicopter. She smelled a man's aftershave, Old Spice? The scent used to make her swoon. Now it was pulling her back to a childhood memory, dressed in dark shadows, voices echoing along a narrow cobblestone road under a moonless sky. Maggie floated into her over-shuffled deck of edited remembrances and fairy tales. A safer space.

"Come on, Moonwalker, we've got to get going. We're going to surprise Maggie."

Tekla grabbed her gray, curly-wool stuffed animal, Windsor Dog, under her arms and closed her eyes. Sam propped Tekla up on the side of her bed and pointed to clothes his Ma and Tekla had laid out for school tomorrow.

"Listen to me. This is important. We've got to get a move on. Uncle Clyde found us a plane to Canada, and if we don't hurry, we'll miss it."

"I can't," Tekla cried, "I've got a spelling bee tomorrow!"

"You can, and you will. There are lots of spelling bees, but maybe only one chance to fly off on a plane and surprise Maggie in Canada! Come on, Moonwalker. We can do this. It'll be a blast."

Tekla crossed her arms and said, "You don't get it—this is like the final championship bee between me and . . ."

"No choice here, little one. We're going to Canada. I need you to keep up with me, follow my directions. It's important—like one of those Eagle Scout survival games. We need to stay perfectly synchronized. Do you know what that means?"

"I know what it means, plus I can spell it, S – Y – N . . ."

"Great! We'll have a spelling bee on the plane, but right now, we've got to move like the wind. Can you do that?"

"Look out, Han Solo," Tekla growled between gritted teeth like the boys on the playground during recess. She pulled her mod jeans on under her nightgown, then pointed to the door for Sam to leave so she could finish dressing.

On their way out, Sam said, "We're going to pretend this is an undercover escape." Holding his finger to his lips, he led Tekla out the screened-in porch, across the backyard and through the weeds to the small gravel road that dead-ended at the creek. A long, black car was idling.

Sam didn't see the drainage ditch until he was on top of it and leapt over. Tekla lost her balance and fell into the murky water: white tennies caked in mud; jeans and coat sleeves soaking wet. Sam looked like he was holding his breath, waiting for Tekla to pitch a fit. Instead, Tekla stretched both her arms out in the starless night, folded her hands, and whispered, "Please save me. My family's totally bonkers."

After helping Tekla out of the ditch, Sam lifted and held her up like a trophy fish. "You got that right."

Jumping out of the limo, Clyde tipped his chauffer's cap and held the back door open for Sam and Tekla.

"Nice touch," said Sam.

"Hey, Moonwalker, you still hanging out with this donkey?"

"Hey, Uncle Clyde, he dragged me out of bed to take me on an EAGLE SCOUT survival game. No kidding, he doesn't even know I'm a girl."

Maggie lost track of time going in and out of her clumsy sleep-induced stupor. When she was conscious, she knew enough to be alarmed, but not alarmed enough to stay awake and think about where she was, why or with whom. Someone must be flying this sky craft, but Maggie no longer heard voices or picked up the scent of Old Spice. Was there a woman with a French accent—no, a woman who spoke French? It might have been a dream or an old memory. Everything seemed so vague, surreal. Even the fabric over her face no longer frightened her. Maybe, she thought, it was better not to see, to sleep, to let someone else be in charge.

Maggie woke to a vertical drop and the excited whirl of propellers. By the jiggle, Maggie knew she was in a helicopter—then wondered at her observation. She'd only flown a few times and never in a chopper. Were her other senses on red alert, covering for her lack of sight, movement, speech? When the cabin door opened, Maggie felt the rush of cold, wet air—not because of rain, but water, a body of water. Planning her escape, Maggie willed herself to memorize every step, sound, shift of wind.

By the time Clyde made it home to pick up Blanche and the boys for this unplanned road-trip to Canada, the Piper Cheyenne flight, scheduled to carry Sam and Tekla, was aborted before take-off. Blanche was holding the telephone receiver when Clyde walked into the kitchen.

"Hey, Sam, what's up?"

"Mechanical problems. According to the mechanic—dash, reservations' clerk, dash, jack-of-all-trades—it looks like we'll be good to go by six a.m., seven at the latest. That's if they can find a pilot. The first guy walked because he wouldn't be back in time for his day job."

"That's crazy. We'll come by and drop you off at the train station in Windsor."

"No, we're good. Tekla's excited about her first flight; we've got the lounge to ourselves, and the vending machines are full. Let's plan for ten a.m. in Hippie Haven."

"Got it; see you then."

By the time Clyde hung up, the three boys and Blanche were in the kitchen grazing, listening in on the late-night call.

"Okay, guys, I know it's last minute, but I need you to pack your bags for a week. We're heading to some good fishing in Canada—Kitchener, maybe Blue Mountain!"

"Dad, no. No way. Friday's the homecoming game and the backup kicker has the Russian Flu. I can't let the team down. I won't!"

Clyde looked at his number one son and didn't know whether he wanted to hug him or take him down a notch, remind him he wasn't in charge. Instead, he pulled in his breath and looked at this young Clyde Webster, his namesake. Tall, strong, good-looking, smart, thoughtful, responsible—his firstborn was a much better, more honest, and courageous person than he'd ever been, would be.

"Look, I get that you want to do the right thing. I respect it. But there's too much you don't know, can't know. If you stay here, you could put your team and us at risk. I know you wouldn't want to take that chance."

"Bullshit," young Clyde whispered.

"Speak up, son. What did you say?

"I said bullshit!"

"Maybe, maybe not. You willing to risk our safety for a field goal?"

Clyde watched his son slide his hands into the front pockets of his khakis, lean over at his waist, then kick Jam's empty dog dish across the kitchen floor with the inside of his right foot.

"What do I tell my coach?"

The wind, alone, was wicked without the help of helicopter propellers stirring up gusts, puddles of water, and sharp pieces of gravel. *Losing track of time and being pelted by stones and cold water was intimidating enough,* thought Maggie, *but terrifying when you couldn't see.* Her initial temptation was to check-out mentally, but she knew her survival depended on staying focused, tuned in. Under the heavy scarf, the night looked black, starless. She guessed it was after midnight but before two a.m., maybe later. The surface under her feet felt hard, roughly paved with scattering, loose debris. On her left, a small hand with a determined grip belonged to a woman. On Maggie's right, a large hand with a light hold signaled someone taller, more confident in hostage-taking skills, a man. Were these the same people from the car? The chopper? Or were they waiting when the helicopter landed? Maggie kept her head down and attempted to keep her body limp—shuffling her walk, stumbling—whatever she could do to lull them into complacency, a slip of the tongue, the name of the town, a way out.

Before the propellers stopped their incessant spinning, Maggie felt the man reach forward and open a door. Metal against metal—a rooftop access door in a city or an abandoned warehouse in the middle of nowhere? Based on the velocity of the wind, Maggie was betting a rooftop in a city close to Hamilton. Toronto? Windsor? Quebec? New York? *Think*, she commanded her meandering brain. How long were they in the air?

"Stairs," said the man, "go slow." Through her cloth mask, the stairwell was an unlit descent through a coal mine. The woman released Maggie's left arm and held back. When Maggie let her knees buckle on the top few steps, the man said, "On your feet, stay up." Maggie ransacked her memory to find his voice. Something about his pronunciation of 'up,' a Canadian? She needed more and let her knees buckle again. This time the man tightened his grip, softened his voice, and said, "Up." A *Canuck*, she thought, and wise to her game.

Maggie wanted to bang her muddled head against the wall. She'd missed her chance to slip off her wedding ring while they were on the roof—a crumb to let roof-searchers know where she was or where she'd met her demise. *Holy mother of god*, she thought, *I'm screwed if I drift off.*

Picking up her count on the fifth step, Maggie ran the tip of her index finger along the left wall; concrete with no coat of paint to smooth the surface; no handrail. The sound of the woman's leather soles, behind them, came from her right and held a regular cadence; a handrail securing her footfalls? After step fifteen, a small concrete landing made a ninety-degree left turn before descending fifteen more steps. Thick carpet cushioned the next landing and Maggie longed to drop to the floor, curl up and sleep—her only reliable means of escape. Instead, she stood quietly and listened as the man used a key to unlock the door. The woman whispered in French, "*Dépêche-toi, je dois faire pipi!*" Maggie didn't recognize the voice, but in English or French, "Hurry, I must pee!" was a

Pavlov's dog whistle for her jostled bladder. Urine scrambled down Maggie's legs as the man guided her through the open door.

*No time for embarrassment,* Maggie thought, as she executed her well-practiced virtual jackknife dive off the high board to restore ice-cold clarity and calm. Picking up the scents, the echoes of their steps, the sound of electric generators, and the movement of wind against windows, she knew this place.

# 7

# Scavenger Hunts

TUESDAY MORNING, SEPTEMBER 20, 1977—"Hey, sleepyhead, no time for a spelling bee in the sky," said Sam. "We're ready to land. You awake?"

Between the noise of the engines, bounce of the wind, and land rushing up to the plane's windshield, Tekla worried she'd throw up, pee her pants, or both. Sam was in the co-pilot's seat and she was strapped in a small seat behind the pilot—watching him play with a half dozen levers and dials as if he didn't know which one to use. Tekla had to restrain herself from kicking the back of Sam's seat for making her leave Windsor Dog at home, for missing the spelling bee, for not sitting next to her. Before the first tear streamed down her face, the pilot cried, "Mayday, mayday, mayday!" as the plane lost power and began to spin out of control.

After dropping off Blanche and the wrecking crew at a safehouse in Kitchener, Ontario, Clyde headed northeast to Toronto as the sun began to color the eastern fringe of Canada. Prepared with maps, compasses, tools, access codes, and emergency contact numbers, he and Sam planned to rendezvous at the Maple Leaf, a small *pensione* in Yorkville—a Toronto neighborhood better known as Hippie Haven. Because Tekla was being left at a safehouse in Vaughan, Ontario, with people she'd never met, Clyde knew the drop-off would take time. Relaxing his foot on the accelerator, Clyde tuned the radio to CKLM—with air space in Detroit, Windsor, and beyond.

"Just off the teletype, we either have a mayday crash or one bodacious emergency landing just short of Maple Airport near Toronto. Fire and rescue crews have been dispatched. Once we know more, we'll give you a shout."

Clyde pulled off the road to collect his thoughts. Unlike Vietnam—where poor, inexperienced foot soldiers fought for black gold under the cloak of god, country, and freedom—this battleground was both smaller and larger. Today, on Canadian soil, his family and Sam's were genomes hitching a ride on a planet being devastated by greed. Chilled by the certainty Sam and Tekla were on that plane, Clyde knew every move counted and any lost minute was blown. Oz agents assigned to Operation Clockwork Orange, who knew Sam and Tekla's ETA at Maple Airport, would be scrambling. Orchestrated plans no longer counted. In an emergency, they relied on knowledge, trust, and the impossibly abstract concept of coordinating through intuition. Easing off the soft shoulder onto the two-lane macadam road, Clyde turned up the radio and began his search for signs of life and a phone booth.

With the teletype clicking in the background, CKLM launched into its regular, often irreverent, *Spot Cast*, "If you haven't heard, Amnesty International won the Nobel Peace Prize, which sounds precious as hell, but who else, right? For those of you looking for a counter-revolution, time to pack your bags and move to Quebec. They just announced their plan to force-feed French as their official language to shut down the separatist rebellion. Good luck with that! Down south, U.S. President Jimmy Carter announced his decision to give away the Panama Canal . . ."

After walking twenty-six steps along a carpeted hallway, Maggie was guided into a hard-surfaced, clunky elevator that stopped three times and sounded an alarm. At each stop, Maggie heard someone punch buttons to silence the alarm and free the elevator to continue its climb. On the fourth stop, the punched buttons led to the sound of a metal gate sliding to the left, and Maggie noted, the slightest change of barometric pressure inside the elevator. Maggie was so certain they were at Zeno Development, Jacques' company in Toronto, that she stopped considering other sites. The problem was Jacques' building was only three stories high. *Think,* she commanded herself, *did I count two or three flights of stairs into the basement before we got on the elevator?* Physically and emotionally exhausted, with urine from her pants and shoes burning her skin, Maggie fought an overwhelming impulse to drop into a fetal position. The man with the Canadian accent said, "Up. Just a few more yards, Marguerite. You're safe." Maggie gritted her teeth and fought back tears.

The first public phone booth turned out to be twenty miles away—out of range for CKLM, out of range for any news radio. Clyde's frustration eased when he heard Blanche's voice answer the phone.

"Hello, George Carver's residence. May I help you?"

"Yes, you can. I need you to listen to me without reacting. Don't ask questions or cry out. I want you to make positive, conversational comments like I see, sure, no problem, okay, of course. This is important."

"Of course."

"I just got word that a plane either crashed or made a forced landing near Maple Airport. That's where Sam and Tekla were landing. I'm not one-hundred percent sure it was their plane, but damn close. We're in emergency mode, and you need to be hyper-alert and keep the kids grounded."

"No problem. We expect some weather tonight, but the boys can't wait to cast their lines in the river after breakfast."

"I'll let you know as soon as I know. In the meantime, stay close to the phone. I'll call every four hours. You may be the only central contact Oz has to coordinate movement, so make a big pot of coffee, answer the phone, keep the kids on a short leash, and trust your fine instincts."

"For sure."

"And don't forget the old Chevy wagon in the shed has a full tank of gas. Keys are hanging under the hammer over the work-bench. If you don't hear from me every four hours, starting now, you and the kids pile into the wagon and take the scenic route to Blue Mountain with your fishing tackle. You know the drill."

"Got it."

"I know you do and love you for it. Stay safe, Mrs. Webster."

"You too, Mr. Webster."

Making a right turn, Maggie counted twelve steps down a carpeted, softly lit hall before they stopped. The man removed his hand from her arm and crossed in front of her. He appeared to be tall, six feet or more. To her left, a door opened, and she heard the click of a light switch before the room brightened. A small hand on her back coaxed her into the room. Speaking English, the woman said, "It's okay, Marguerite. You're safe now. I'll help you clean up and get settled."

With her face still covered in fabric, Maggie saw the outline of the man standing next to a bed. He said, "I know you're freaked and have many questions. But first, you sleep and let the drugs wear off. No one will bother you tonight. In the morning, a woman you've never met will enter your room and introduce herself. She'll be your guide."

Maggie forced words through her parched vocal cords, "No. Please. Tell me now. I need to know who you are. Why I'm here."

Walking past her the man turned before he opened the door, held his hands up as if in supplication, and said, "Mrs. Tervo, our existentialist talks will have to wait until you're off drugs and rested—until then, we need to run some here-and-now traps."

After the door closed, Maggie scanned the room through her scarf, more desperate than ever for a place to curl up or disappear. Before throwing herself on the bed, she remembered her urine-soaked pants and stopped herself. The woman touched Maggie's right shoulder, then began to untie and unwrap the scarf. When she finished, the woman handed Maggie the scarf—the same scarf worn by the woman in the back of the bar at the Royal Connaught Hotel.

"Marguerite, my name's Bernadette. French is my first language, but I've been recast as an American. If you don't mind, we'll stick to English—or as my mother calls it, Amerlish. In the real world, I'm a psychiatric nurse. I've been with Oz for almost eight years. My job here is to help new members make the transition to our double life—dealing with the exits and re-entries of our so-called ordinary lives. Last night was an Orange Alert—second only to Red. My first emergency, I was told we don't normally use drugs, blindfolds, and helicopters to move people around. You must be exhausted."

Bernadette and Maggie looked at each other without any apparent signs of recognition or comradery. Yet, Maggie was sure they both experienced the inevitability and significance of their connection. A psychological hook, Maggie let loose her pent-up tears and accepted Bernadette's hug.

"Of course, you're scared out of your mind, who wouldn't be? This is hard stuff—but don't go numb. Stay alert, Marguerite. I promise you're safer here than you'd be anywhere."

Stepping back and studying Maggie's face, Bernadette's voice took on a more upbeat, officious tone. "Let's get you showered and into bed. You might think you won't sleep, but you will. The drugs we gave you have a rebound effect. This afternoon, the world will look more like a friend, and you'll meet Carla, your first guide."

Grabbing a pair of white pajamas from a small cabinet, Bernadette tossed them on the bed. Walking to the other side of the room, she drew open a white canvas drape and exposed the tiny European-styled loo—white tile walls and floor, lidless toilet, lipless washbasin, and a showerhead that drained into the center of the bathroom floor.

In less than two minutes, Maggie stripped off her clothes, grabbed a white towel off the rack, and turned the shower on full blast. With the sting of hot water against her skin, she closed her eyes and sent a silent prayer: *Please, god, if there is one, if you're there, if you're listening, let Tekla and Sam be safe.*

# 8

# Candles in the Rain

TUESDAY MORNING, SEPTEMBER 20, 1977—"I always thought Merriam was a girl," said Maggie.

Carla looked up and asked, "Merriam?"

"You know, Merriam-Webster. I thought Merriam was a girl, and Webster was a boy. Made me giddy to think a girl wrote the dictionary and decided she must've been smarter than Webster because her name came first. I was crushed to learn Merriam was the last name of two brothers, George and Charles Merriam—printers and booksellers who bought the rights to Noah Webster's life work and had the audacity to take top billing."

"You're a weird one, Marguerite."

"Guilty as charged. I have no idea why that obscure bit of trivia showed up as a conversation starter. Please call me Maggie. Marguerite's way too formal for a weirdo."

From the bistro table, hosting coffee cups, fresh fruit, and croissants, Maggie took in the room, or cell—she wasn't sure which.

Fixed metal blinds on the windows blocked the view and projected narrow slats of gray shadow against white-washed walls and bedding. Maggie was wearing a complimentary white terry-cloth robe over her complimentary white pajamas and bare feet.

Across the table, Carla looked uncomfortable in a navy-blue suit, navy pumps, and a crisp white button-down shirt. Small hipped and thin from the waist down, the straight-cut shirt and jacket were working overtime to contain enormous breasts. *Guide my ass*, thought Maggie. She was sure the 'interview suit' was intended to make a statement, add a touch of decorum to the brute force used to abduct her.

"So, Carla, how did you get hooked up with Oz?"

"Jacques Ruivivar and I go way back. We did some counter-intelligence work for the CIA in Cuba during the mid-sixties—helped Oz fill in some blanks."

"Do you know my husband Sam, Sam Tervo?"

Carla picked up her coffee, took a sip, and peered at Maggie over the cup. Finally, she said, "I can't say I *know* Sam. We met when we were both working at Sheer Juice. I worked days; he worked nights. It was rare for us to run into each other."

"Huh . . . interesting. Carla was the name of the administrative assistant who seduced Sam in the conference room the night before we got married."

Carla put down her cup, rolled her shoulders back, then closed her eyes before she looked at Maggie and said, "One and the same. All mob-driven—*La Bière* and their gang of thieves. I worked both sides. Nothing happened. The sex thing, videotape—smoke and mirrors."

The sound of a generator made its way through the pause. Maggie leaned forward and spoke in a slow, clipped whisper, "What do you mean? Are you saying you set Sam up, put this whole thing in motion?"

"Me? No way. I'm a minion; I listen, follow directions, and keep my head down. Based on what I've heard, the whole thing started when Sam gave Clyde a lift from the Freedom Rider's digs to Angelo's Pizzeria, years before he worked at Sheer Juice. Oz vets its members five or more years before putting them in the field. This week would have been your orientation, but when you hooked *La Bière* into the mix, the wheels came off an entire fleet of Boeing 747 Jumbo Jets. Jacques can give you the details. I'm here because I know the juicers we're dealing with, and I can teach you the ropes. Like it or not, last night, you were body-blocked on Oz's wobbly-ass bridge. We can cross it together, or you can jump off at any point, any time. The rub is post-jump options become fewer and farther between with each passing day. What you can't do is go rogue and risk Oz's work or its people."

"Did I do that when I set off *La Bière*?"

"I have no idea. Jacques and Catherine make those calls."

"If someone goes rogue, what then?"

"They disappear."

Maggie's head turned to the door, then the window, then back again. She knew she was standing on the edge of a bottomless abyss. Maybe the same abyss her parents faced.Were the few creature comforts—a hot shower, sleep, coffee, a fresh croissant, dry clothes, and a friendly voice—enough to get people to let down their guard? Choose submissiveness over self-will? Pushing back her chair, Maggie was having a hard time catching her breath but understood the need to act. Standing up, hands on the table, she leaned forward, her face inches from Carla. Maggie's tongue felt thick, and a thunderous roar in her ears caused her voice to sound light-years away. "What do you mean they disappear? Are they forced? How?" Taking a deep breath, Maggie pressed her voice beyond the roar, crying, "How? How do you know? Answer me!"

Carla backed her chair away from the table and spoke in a quiet, measured voice, "They're gone, Maggie. Because of our security plan, no one talks about members or speaks their full names when they're here, so it's hard to know they're gone. But, at some point, we notice that they no longer show up in the usual places, the periodic meetings. My guess is the way they disappear is different for everyone. Oz avoids predictability like the plague. It's the death knell."

# 9

# Blinded by the Light

TUESDAY MORNING, SEPTEMBER 20, 1977—Southern-style—the covered front porch of the two-story, reclaimed-brick house in Kitchener had always been Blanche's favorite space in Canada. Perched on one of six weary, mismatched rockers on the wide-plank deck, Blanche had a clear view of the gravel road and easy access to the coffee pot and phone through the screen door. When she caught sight of orange and gold mums in clay pots trimming each of the three steps, it looked like someone lived there. Blanche half smiled and shook her head—a nice touch by Oz's staging crew.

Although Blanche grooved on the buzz of Detroit—the magic of Motown, its energy and opportunities—she revered the sound of silence, Paul Simon's vibe. That morning the chill air swaggered with chlorophyll as if mocking the sun-flashed yellow leaves. In the distance, a barndoor groaned and a buck shot out of the woods—galloping across the front yard, scattering birds and squirrels. For just a tick, Blanche lost herself in a fairy-tale world—*grandmother, what big ears you have*—then pulled herself up. Images of Sam, Maggie, and Tekla were everywhere—too vast to amend or ignore, too loud to distill into silence.

Ninety percent of the time, Blanche thought of Oz as a social club, sometimes only a concept or goal. But when the other ten percent hit, the hardcore stakes, costs, and risks eliminated any doubt about Oz's purpose. In the early days, there were times when she thought about bolting. No more. International corporate behemoths were pillaging and poisoning the planet. First and third-world nations were being bought and sold on private yachts, jets, and golf carts. *Belly up to the bar boys and get yourself an ambassadorship, maybe a chair, a judgeship, or one of those get-out-of-jail-free cards for money laundering, racketeering, mayhem, murder.* Blanche's foot was tapping out an angry beat when the phone rang.

Slamming through the screen door, Blanche stopped, took a deep breath, found her southern-style cadence, and said, "Hello, George Carver's Residence. May I help you?"

"Blanche, Loretta here. Are you okay? Free to talk?"

"Oh, god. I'm relieved to hear your voice. The boys are out back fishing. What can you tell me?"

"Nothing. I'm calling because I can't find Sam or Clyde. Where is everyone?"

"Hold on," said Blanche as she peered out the window over the kitchen sink and saw the boys at the riverbank. Clyde Jr. was casting and recasting his first fiberglass fishing pole. Clive, the next in line to inherit their four-figure passbook savings account, was stretched out on the grass with a transistor radio next to his ear, tapping out a beat on his chest. And their baby, thirteen-year-old Carter, was sitting cross-legged under a tree reading a tattered copy of Orwell's *1984*.

After Blanche told Loretta about her call with Clyde, the line went quiet. "Loretta? You still there?"

"Part of me is. We need to keep the line clear for Clyde. When he calls, ask him to call me. In the meantime, I'll try some back numbers to reach Jacques. You, my sister-friend, take care of yourself and the boys. Is Marmalade there to keep watch? Sorry, I mean Jam. Is he just as protective as Marmalade?"

"We think so—but border crossing with a dog takes planning. He's with my mom."

"Well, then, keep the watch and stay awake."

"You too, Loretta. Call if you find out anything. Clyde says they're in emergency mode, acting on instinct and intuition. I'm the contact point."

"Is your radio on?"

"No. I didn't want the boys to hear, but damnit to hell, Clive's out back listening to his transistor. Talk later."

"The death knell?" asked Maggie, her words breaking through a weariness that felt more like defeat. Mirroring Carla's quiet, measured tempo, she said, "Listen to me. I have a husband and a child. I want to go home now. Right now. If I can't use the phone, I want you to call Sam. You call and tell him to come pick me up."

"Sorry, Maggie. That's not going to happen. Right now, Sam and Tekla are at a higher risk than you. Once we mitigate the risk, going home might be an option. But for now, you're the kryptonite. Containing you and keeping you safe is the only way to keep them safe."

Sinking into her chair, Maggie looked as if she'd disappeared in her body or fled to some otherworldly plane. Then, both her knees began to pulsate as she pulled her hair back and turned, twined, knotted, and lifted it, repeatedly, as if she could force it into a twist.

Carla watched Maggie struggle for a few minutes before she leaned across the table, touched her elbow, and said, "Maggie stop. Please stop. I'll help. You'll be okay."

When Maggie glanced across the table, she saw Carla lean back, nod her head, tighten her mouth, and look away.

"Oh, god," whispered Maggie, "Anna and Raymond were contained."

Clyde's call came minutes after Loretta hung up. He didn't wait for Blanche's greeting.

"Listen close. There's no way I can get near the plane, and Oz hasn't been able to reach anyone who knows if the plane crashed or made an emergency landing. According to the few gawkers, no one's seen or heard an ambulance. I haven't talked to Jacques, but Catherine's at Zeno's holding down the fort. She said if this was the juicers, they moved with lightning speed—which means they took Maggie's impromptu research as a serious threat. Mrs. Webster, I don't see any way to dumb this down. If someone messed with the plane, Catherine and Jacques will upgrade the alert to red. I say we don't wait. You and the boys need to load up the Chevy and head north."

"What's the risk if we don't?"

"Three sons and their remarkable mother."

Blanche was the staid one among The Eights, the one who didn't cry at funerals and never panicked when someone crashed their car, broke a limb, or landed in jail. She was well-known for dark humor. But this was far too dark, too close. "And you, Mr. Webster. What about you?"

"Call Catherine when you get there. She'll let me know."

# 10

# Right Place, Wrong Time

HIGH NOON TUESDAY, SEPTEMBER 20, 1977—The sun was straight up, and the door locked, when Clyde reached Zeno Development. After using two keys to open the deadbolts, he entered the empty lobby and found Emma's legendary bilingual note tucked under the phone on her reception desk:

> Chers Visiteurs et Cambrioleurs,
>
> Je suis sortie déjeuner. Si vous avez besoin d'aide, applelez la sécurité par l'interphone, s'il vous plait.
>
> Merci beaucoup, Emma Stell
>
> Dear Visitors and Burglars,
>
> I'm out having a lovely lunch. Please press the intercom button to reach security for help.
>
> Many thanks, Emma Stell

On any other day, Clyde would have bounded up the steps to Catherine's office. Today, he buzzed security to let them know he was in the lobby before he dragged his weary bones up two flights.

Lunch was sitting on the coffee table in the small anteroom outside Catherine and Jacques' offices. Clyde fingered the bags of sandwiches, dill pickles, chips and Coke without an appetite. He was sure Zeno's kitchen closed because 'nonessential personnel' were relieved from duty during an Orange Alert. Loretta went bat-shit the first time she heard Jacques use the term 'nonessential personnel.' She called it a white-man-walking euphemism—racist, classist, sexist. In pure Jacques' style, he confessed his ignorance and apologized.

With Blanche and the crew heading out of Dodge, Clyde took time to tap down his irritation for being ordered to leave the airport. Although he fought it, he knew a big black guy hanging out at a private airport in a white burb was like a flashing neon sign. If he wanted to find Sam and Tekla, he'd have to go undercover. Out the window, Lake Ontario's far-most horizon lost itself in dazzling blue strata. Clyde whispered, "If you're so god-damn almighty, bring it on." It was as close to a prayer as he was willing to offer some sanctimonious savior in the sky.

"Catherine, you there?"

Catherine walked out and gave Clyde a hug that lingered until Clyde caught Jacques' eyes.

Jacques looked down, shook his head, and said, "No word. If they suspect foul play, the Security Service will get involved. Talk about the fox guarding the henhouse. The Security Service is the intelligence arm of the Royal Canadian Mounted Police. After getting a blank check to crush Quebec's separatist movement, these cops in trench coats have been flexing their muscle with new badges, a secret handshake, and unchecked bravado."

"Do we know if the plane crashed or not? Survivors . . . or not?" asked Clyde.

"Don't know. Without the sirens as a signal, there's always the possibility they were removed quietly to avoid a second strike against them. That means they could be alive in a safe house set up by the Mounties, *La Bière*, others."

"Are we searching for them?"

Catherine looked up from unwrapping a pastrami sandwich and said, "We've got our best undercover agents hitting the streets. Based on what we know, I'm sure they're alive. No one from Canada made a long-distance call to the Livonia number, and unless something happened in the last ten minutes, the cops in Livonia haven't dispatched anyone to check the house. The Canadian dicks must know Maggie's in Canada."

"What about Sam's mother? Anyone check with Maija?" asked Clyde.

"Too risky. We've got Pete set up to call her for a friendly chat and see if she offers anything. She's savvy."

"I thought Maija and Pete broke it off."

"They did, six or seven times, but they keep talking. The worst case is someone from the CIA is keeping Maija company till the dust settles. Let's see," said Catherine, looking at her watch, "hmm, five minutes until our next update. How's Blanche?"

"She's heading north with the 'wrecking crew' and fishing gear. Do we have someone stationed at Blue Mountain?"

Jacques scanned the room before he locked eyes with Clyde, smiled, and said, "Beats me. Did someone call a Red Alert?"

Clyde nodded. "I know—I jumped the gun. But things were flying off the radar, and my gut said *run with it*, so I did."

"Your gut?" Jacques exploded, "We've got a downed plane, missing passengers, a combative hostage, two dead hitmen at the Royal Connaught, and your gut told you to run with it? What if your gut just sent your wife and three boys into an ambush?"

"Enough, Jacques," said Catherine, "there's no way to predict the next attack. All it means is we have one less safehouse to keep safe. If we think no one knows about the Kitchener house, or Vaughan house, or any other safehouse, it's time to turn in our Dick Tracey watches. Loretta and Bruce are at Blue Mountain running some traps. I'll let them know to expect Blanche and the boys."

Clyde looked from Catherine to Jacques, then down at his hands to find he was cracking his knuckles for the first time since he went AWOL. "Jacques is right. With the sound of Vietnam drumming in my head, I lost it and put everyone at risk. Next time I hear those drums . . ."

Jacques touched Clyde's arm and said, "Let it go, my friend. What's done is done. God knows you've seen more combat than anyone. If we can't trust your gut, we're toast. I was wrong."

With Jacques' unkempt look and obvious fatigue, Clyde wondered if he'd aged over the last several months or just the past few hours. It didn't matter. He cleared his voice to ask the question taking up most of the oxygen in the room, "How's Maggie?"

A rush of air—Jacques' held breath and bound tension—seemed to expand the small space. A full minute passed before he looked up and said, "The abduction ripped her apart, me apart, Catherine apart. But Marguerite? Ah. Tough as nails that one." Looking at Catherine, he dropped his voice, "No doubt, she's got her mother's courage and knows how to keep it together. But no way we can sit down with her until we find Sam and Tekla. She'll know something's off."

Catherine bit her lower lip and shook her head. "You're wrong about Maggie being tough. Carla said she was sucker-punched today when she thought her parents disappeared because they went rogue. We know the truth, Maggie doesn't."

Jacques sat forward, as if he was about to challenge Catherine, then looked at her like good friends do when awe gets in the way of anger. Clyde never understood why they didn't marry, but whatever kept them together, connected them, fueled Oz to accomplish goals far beyond the stated and imagined. So far beyond, they were often called to help Oz's world organization defend against developing autocracies—to upend precarious dictators and dismantle the stream of first-world claims for the mineral and oil rights, airspace, and waterways of developing and third-world countries.

When the phone rang, Catherine waved Clyde into the office. Jacques hit the speaker button and said, "Catherine, Clyde, and Jacques here. Who's calling?"

"Marc here. Just got off the horn with a couple of airport mechanics. You might want to sit down."

"Go ahead," said Jacques, "we're sitting around Catherine's desk staring at the speaker. What do you have?"

"The good news is a little girl and two men might be sitting down for lunch after their plane dropped out of the sky. The rest of the story is freaking crazy. According to the mechanics, the Commonwealth's Security Service must've been onsite when the plane hit the ground. Almost immediately, they tagged it an emergency landing—a colossal departure from standard procedure. Typically, the Civil Aviation Directorate makes the call. If there's any suspicion of foul play, the Mounties do their thing before Security Service even decides to weigh in. Now, the story gets more bizarre. Before the fire and rescue crews began to check the plane or examine the pilot and passengers for injuries, no, let me restate that—before the fire and rescue crews even got out of their vehicles—they were turned away.

"The most radical breach was when the pilot and passengers were immediately loaded into a black van and transported to who-knows-where. No one we talked to knew whether the black van reached them after the plane touched down, or if it was parked on that nondescript patch of earth waiting for a UFO or mayday flight. The black van, its driver, and passengers still MIA."

# 11

# Calliope Crashes

TUESDAY AFTERNOON, SEPTEMBER 20, 1977—"Consider this. Calliope, the muse of epic poetry, shares her name with the screeching pipe-organ on a merry-go-round," said Maggie.

"Your point is?" asked Carla.

"My point is there is *no* point. We pretend to find beauty in words, names, ideas—our greedy minds gobbling up another tasty noun, verb, or adjective for a moment of pleasure. Huh! Then what? Our brightly colored, imaginary merry-go-round begins splitting the air with noise as wooden horses gather speed, and the calliope goes berserk trying to keep up. We crash to the ground and think, hmm, this must be beauty."

"Maggie, acting insane isn't going to work."

Maggie swung her right arm open as if inviting guests into her home. "Let's talk about insanity: keeping me locked up in a white cell, ripping families apart, kidnapping friends, seducing a co-worker the night before his wedding day."

"I got it. You're ticked-off. But this time, you set off the calliope and put yourself, Sam, Tekla, Clyde, and almost everyone you know, at risk. I get that you didn't intend this, but whatever you call it, this crash is now our reality and your reality. Tonight, at dinner, someone will come by to talk with you, give you more information. The shopping bag next to the door has some street clothes and shoes, plus the Moleskine notebook, pencils, and two books you asked for."

Maggie held her hands in a prayer position, bent at the waist, and said, "Namaste."

Carla bowed her head, smiled, and looked at Maggie with a tenderness Maggie hadn't noticed before. In response, Maggie's heart seemed to physically expand in gratitude before shock set in. After Patty Hearst's rescue from the Symbionese Liberation Army, and her trial for crimes she committed under SLA control, Maggie had become transfixed by the *Stockholm Syndrome*—the disturbing psychology between captors and captives. For Patty Hearst, it meant wielding an automatic weapon during a bank robbery. For Maggie, her over-the-top gratefulness for a few ordinary items and a kind face set off earsplitting alarms.

Maggie returned Carla's smile, wiped an imaginary tear from her right eye, and stepped forward to hug her. Carla stiffened, then relaxed. Maggie realized it was time she became the muse and calliope. Exploiting the SLA's methodology, she'd orchestrate the words and pace by writing her version of a reverse, maybe adverse, Stockholm Syndrome to keep her captors off balance.

Sam's manic relief at surviving the mayday landing was short-lived. By the time they were helped from the plane and loaded into a black van, Sam knew this was pure blockbuster, high-risk theater. Who had the balls and funds to fake a crash-landing and kidnapping in the light of day next to an airport?

The pilot, Nick Morel, grabbed shotgun as he and Tekla were rushed through the van's side door. With a privacy shield behind the front seat and no windows in the back, the calf-trail gravel roads' twists and turns made it impossible to gauge direction. Twenty minutes into the drive, they made a pitstop on a tractor path in the middle of a cornfield.

When Sam saw Tekla's alarm, he lifted her in his arms and whispered, "It's okay. Just walk out a few yards and squat down to pee. No one will see you."

Holding on to his neck with an iron grip, Tekla said, "No! I don't have to pee."

"I think you do. We might be in the car for a long time."

"I'm not going to pee in the weeds."

"Cornstalks, not weeds. There's nowhere else. It's like camping."

Tekla began to squeeze back tears.

"Okay, let's think about this. Where do you want to pee?"

"Behind the car."

"Because?"

"Because a snake might bite my butt in the weeds."

"Ah, I see. Let me check."

Sam raised his right hand, his index finger up, and said, "Gentlemen, the young lady would prefer some privacy behind the van. Would you mind turning your heads for a few minutes?"

"No problem," said the driver as he and Nick turned their heads.

Sam pointed at Tekla and said, "You're good to go. I'll keep watch to make sure no one looks, and no snake even *thinks* about crossing the tractor ruts."

Tekla shook her head as she walked behind the van; Sam smiled at her predictable dismay with the adult world. Somehow Tekla knew that grown-ups perpetuated mindless drama because they had nothing better to do. And standing in the fresh air trying to make sense of the last six hours, Sam saw how futile, overwhelming, and childish it was to think anyone could change the world without hurting others. *What sort of crooked game, crooked god, crooked civilization was at work here?* For now, his focus was on getting to Toronto. As Jacques liked to say, *existentialist incursions will have to wait.*

Jacques walked into the anteroom and said, "That's it! We've got to sit down with Maggie and bring this ancestral masquerade to an end. After that, we'll get F. Lee Bailey—the best lawyers money can buy—to set up a meeting with the Secret Service and CIA. All cards on the table. Done!"

Clyde and Catherine looked up. They'd been contacting Oz agents, manning the phones, checking on leads, hoping to talk with possible witnesses. So far no one knew or was willing to say why a black van scooped up three people from a near-plane-crash and vanished into the day. After the Mounties and Secret Service refused to comment, Clyde and Catherine called everyone they knew who had contacts with the Secret Service, Mounties, MI5, MI6 or CIA, and came up empty.

Holding her hand up, Catherine said, "Whoa! Let's talk. What do you mean by 'done?' You think bringing this masquerade to an end will make us safe? Secure our future? What? Tell me what you think will happen if we lay our cards on the table."

Jacques was used to Catherine challenging him, but today it felt more brutal because he was completely stumped; she knew he was puffing and posturing. They'd spent decades divining this story, tweaking the words, times, places. Truth hadn't eluded them, they'd buried it, rewrote history, and manifested new realities. Now Jacques wanted to revive the truth they'd worked so hard to shed. Jacques held up both hands and said, "Shoot me! I have no earthly idea how we do it, but we must. Somehow we must."

Tapping the eraser end of her pencil against her forehead, Catherine looked at Clyde before she turned to Jacques, "What if we pull out a few cards before we talk to Maggie?"

"Go on," said Jacques.

"The Raymond and Jo cards can wait; they're emotional distractions. We want Maggie focused on Sam and Tekla."

"Really? You think the rest of the story's not an emotional distraction?

"Good point."

"That's it? We meet with Maggie and put all the cards on the table?"

"No, that's not it. After we talk to Maggie, we go for broke and put all the cards on the big table—for everyone to see. We've been shadow boxing all these years, living in the opaque light of some mind-numbing deferred power because we thought we posed too big a threat. All this time, we held power and authority but didn't act. Instead, we let ourselves become immobilized by the fear of retaliation, exposure. We squandered our power while the juicers were poisoning children, then lacked the courage to expose our shameful involvement. Instead of casting light on the threat, we retreated into a deep, dark cave. The three of us have talked about this before, but we've run out of time and deeper caves. We don't know who's holding Tekla and Sam hostage. Over the next twenty-four hours, I want to send copies of everything we have on *La Bière* and the juicers—including Anna's hidden records—to the Mounties, Secret Service, CIA, MI6. Jacques and I will cover this with Oz's leadership. After that, we hit the major news services.

"We'll get Charles to pull together the kitchen and housekeeping staff to set up Zeno space for work and sleep. Bruce can schedule his meetings with the authorities here. Besides, we'll want him to cover the office—address questions, deal with legal challenges, etcetera. Clyde, you take the lead on preparing for the media blitz. Carla, Bernadette, and Emma can work with the printers, binders, and shippers. After the news services, we'll send copies to the big city newspapers in Canada and the States; then, we'll clock how long it takes to make headlines in Hell, Michigan.

"Tonight . . . um . . . huh . . . when we meet with Maggie." Catherine wiped her eyes before continuing. "Let's see . . . tonight we'll tell Maggie that Sam and Tekla are missing. Then we start ripping the doors wide open. Stunning, isn't it? We locked ourselves in, held ourselves hostage, and called it a revolution."

# 12

# The Richter Scale

TUESDAY AFTERNOON, SEPTEMBER 20, 1977—The small mirror over the bathroom sink wasn't intended to provide a full-length view, and the opportunity for metaphor wasn't lost on Maggie. Most of her life had been some warped scientific study in sectioning the physical, emotional, and mental bodies of her unabridged female-specimen-self. Then, years trying to piece back the discordant sections in someone else's vanity mirror. Today, the face looking back at her resembled the girl, woman, wife, mother, lover of her earlier selves, but it was just a mask: a motionless mouth, empty eyes. Maggie knew tonight's performance as the obliged, devoted, compliant captive had to be convincing.

The complimentary clothes and 'Stockholm' gifts Carla dropped off covered the bed: black polyester bell-bottoms, turtleneck and flatties; white underpants and bra; plus, one Moleskine notebook with three sharpened pencils in an unused interoffice envelope. The *coup de grâce* sat on the bed stand: two books Maggie had been longing to read—*One Hundred Years of Solitude*, by

Gabriel Garcia Márquez and *Our Bodies, Ourselves,* by the Boston Women's Health Book Collective. The irony was too much. From some unexplored corner of Maggie's dissected bio-self, a giggle formed, grew, and grew, until it exploded into gut-wrenching, side-splitting belly laughs before the flood gates opened.

"Where do we start? Better yet, who starts?"

Catherine looked at Jacques and realized he, too, was strung out about their meeting with Maggie. For decades they avoided this potential face-off because to do otherwise would have immobilized them. *No,* thought Catherine, *to do otherwise would have disembodied them—turned them into zombies.* Why did she think this was such a good idea a few hours ago? They had no clue what the fallout would be, who would get caught in the crossfire, who might crash and burn. She and Jacques had spent decades writing and rewriting potential scripts. But now, here they were, ready to walk into a room with Maggie, without an outline, cheat-sheet, or note-card to guide them.

"After a lifetime of anticipation, scripting, and re-scripting, we're cliff jumping. Oz thinks it's time. We think it's time. And god knows, Maggie was ready to go this alone. You and I don't do trust well. We like to check and recheck. But my love—partner in crime and other escapades of the soul—when the rope bridge swings like a trapeze, it's up to us to hold on."

Jacques brushed Catherine's hair away from her eyes and said, "I know . . . we have no choice. Seventeen years ago, it seemed like the only way to protect our families, avoid the madness and mayhem. Now, we're paying the price."

"You start. Let Maggie know we're ready for the long conversation. If you move too quickly, I'll slow you down or add my perspective. Then, when I tell my story, you can do the same for me. I'm afraid I'll try to rush, get it out before I lose courage."

"Not a chance you'll lose courage. The bigger risk is we get sloppy and maudlin. Our actions might feel like an *avant-garde* leap off the cliff, but external factors forced our hand. We're in danger, Sam and Tekla are in danger. What we say, how we say it, and the actions we take will affect all of us. Tonight, we keep our attention on Maggie; make sure she understands us, and we understand her."

Catherine took a deep breath. Although Jacques tried to downsize the threat by focusing on tonight's conversation, she knew it was impossible to shrink the magnitude of this encounter. There was no Richter Scale for these kinds of quakes.

At six o'clock, Maggie heard a knock before someone called out "dinner service" and used a key to unlock the door. A middle-aged man in a white chef's jacket stood in the hall.

"*Excusez-moi, Mademoiselle.* Sorry for the interruption. I was asked to set up your room for dinner and let you know two others will be joining you at six-thirty."

Following her earlier bout of unbridled laughter and tears, Maggie had focused on ways to upset the captor-captive power imbalance and disarm her caretakers. Prepared for her first test, Maggie jumped off the edge of her bed and assumed the role of the haughty grand dame. Waving her arms toward the table, she smiled brightly and said, "*Bonsoir, Monsieur! Entrez s'il vous plait.*"

After wheeling in a linen-draped food-service cart, with a warming tray and small beverage bar, the porter began setting the table. With as much improv authority as Maggie could muster, she edged past him and lifted the top of the warming tray. Inhaling the *boeuf bourguignon,* she dipped the serving spoon into the sauce, tasted it, and exclaimed, "Mmm . . . excellent!"

Instead of turning around, the porter kept his eyes on her as he backstepped his way to the door, nodded, and said, "*Bon appétit, mademoiselle.*"

Looking for signs of compassion, curiosity, interest—there were none. Maggie wondered if these kinds of meals were ordinary. How many prisoners had he served in this room, in this building? With forced *joie de vivre*, Maggie exclaimed, "*Merci beaucoup, Monsieur!*" Then, she began to wave with rampant enthusiasm, as if the poor man was standing on the third deck of an ocean liner during its prolonged blast before departure.

Momentarily tempted to consider this her first effort at a reverse-Stockholm offensive, Maggie was not delusional. This over-acted, clichéd exchange with the porter was a fiasco. No doubt he'd report her as a nut case.

Maybe she was. After all, who in their right mind would think they could act out a scene and flip reality? The anticipation and energy of the night weren't calling on lovers to sweep across a chandeliered ballroom to the sound of Frank Sinatra. Oh, no! This night called for exotic wedding dancers on broken plates in the basement of a Greek Church—locking arms, moving in a frenzy—as Zorba cranks the tempo faster and faster.

# 13

# The Dinner

TUESDAY EVENING, SEPTEMBER 20, 1977—Minutes before she heard the elevator bell at six-thirty, Maggie realized she didn't have the ovaries to attempt a reverse-Stockholm offensive. Every bone and muscle in her body was tense with insecurity and neediness. If it wasn't Jacques and Catherine, Maggie had to believe it was someone whose benevolent authority would free her from this Orwellian dystopia and return her to Sam and Tekla.

Maggie knew tonight promised to be one of those otherworldly events that halts time, catches one's breath, and preserves itself as a big-screen epic. But this wasn't her show; she'd have to wing it. Instead of cunning and steel, Maggie would be the passive observer. Whoever showed up would have to do the heavy lifting. She'd take her cues from them.

Sitting on the edge of her neatly tucked mattress, Maggie listened as the key entered the lock and unlatched the bolt. With the hair on her arms rising, she fought an impulse to scurry off the other side of the bed as Catherine entered the room. When Jacques walked in, Maggie heard the most unbearable wail escape her lips before she began chanting, "No, no, no, no!"

Stopping inside the door, Jacques' said, "My beautiful Marguerite, I'm so sorry. Please stop. We're here to help. No one's going to hurt you."

Catherine sat next to Maggie and took her hands. "Shh, shh, shh . . . you're okay," she whispered. "Maggie, we need you to listen. As evil as this must feel, does feel, we had to take you against your will because of an abundance of love, caution, and concern for your life and everyone else's. It might feel like it's too much to take in, but we're running out of time. Sam and Tekla need you to be strong right now. Before the sun sets tomorrow, everyone will know the truth. We have less than twenty-four hours to dismantle and rebuild almost three decades. You deserve the truth, and we're prepared to tell you everything we can in as little time as it takes. Later you'll have time to rage, but not now. Now, my brave girl, we set the world back on its axis."

Maggie pulled away from Catherine and looked at her, then Jacques. "Why do Sam and Tekla need me to be strong? Where are they?"

"We have every reason to believe they're safe, but right now, we don't know where they are. According to Clyde, they boarded a private plane in Detroit and arrived in Toronto this morning. The plane either faked—or was forced to make—an emergency landing. We aren't sure which. Witnesses said an unmarked black van whisked them away. Oz agents are combing the countryside, following up on every lead. There's a strong possibility the van belongs to Canada's Secret Service. If not, it may be a scheme by *La Bière* to pressure Oz to back off. Sam and Tekla need our help," said Jacques.

Maggie's eyes darted toward the door, then to Jacques, finally back to Catherine. Maggie expected her familiar ice-cold clarity to take over, to give her strength. But there was nothing to hang on to. Her worst fears were waiting for her to show up—to be fierce, competent, resourceful. To be the heroine of her masterpiece theater, not this pathetic shell of flesh and blood doubled over in grief.

When her tears subsided, Maggie sat up. Both Jacques and Catherine were leaning toward her in worry—clashing with the savory, celebratory smell of dinner. There are no other words thought Maggie—*Sam and Tekla need our help*. The weight of inaction was too much to bear. "Okay, I know we've got to eat. But I don't want to stop for anything, especially a meal. Can we keep working? Get some Coke or coffee and munch on crackers, cheese, salami, grapes, whatever?"

"Done," said Jacques.

By the time the porter arrived to exchange the food carts, Jacques had walked Maggie through everything they knew and didn't know about Sam and Tekla. Then Catherine outlined their plan to expose everything they know about *La Bière* and the juicers—including the US-Canadian cross-border scheme in handling DEPC as an industrial cleaner; intelligence agencies who failed to investigate, ignored facts or accepted payoffs; and the sealing of court records in Chicago and Detroit for the same set of reasons. Catherine ended by saying, "No one wanted to go up against the mob, juicers and power mongers, including Oz."

"While children got sick and died?" asked Maggie.

"Yes," said Catherine, "while children got sick and died. When everything we said we believed in got lost in some demented chariot race for power."

"You can't do this! What if the juicers have Sam and Tekla when the truth hits the streets?"

"That's the point," said Jacques. "We kept quiet all these years because we thought we were protecting you, Sam, Tekla, and others by using Oz's *leverage* as a threat. When we did, we gave our power away and became complicit by hiding the truth. The truth may not set us free in the conventional meaning of freedom. But it took me, us, a lifetime to realize the crippling toll of disguises, pretense, half-truths, lies. What is freedom without the ability to express who we are and what we know? My dear Marguerite, you're about to be slammed by truth."

Loretta was finishing up the dishes when the phone rang.

"Hello, Blue Mountain Retreats, may I help you?"

"Hey, Loretta. Clyde here, how's the crew?"

"Quiet, except for three games of War the boys talked me into playing last night. Seriously, I had no idea cards could be so effing brutal! I'm hiding out in the kitchen."

"Just say no or wipe the floor with them. They're ruthless when it comes to competition in any form, especially when they think they have an easy mark. Did Bruce take off?"

"He did—secretively—because the boys wouldn't give him breathing room. What's up?"

"With Sam and Tekla missing, the Orange Alert's still on. I'm on borrowed time because we're working all night on our response. Is Blanche in easy reach?"

"She is! Hold on."

"Mr. Webster, you okay?"

"Worried about Sam and Tekla, but okay. How's it going there?"

"The boys aren't thrilled about being here without a white person. Carter's convinced that five black people in a white-pine A-frame on Blue Mountain spells trouble."

"What's he reading?"

"1984."

"His instincts are good. Stay inside. I'm sure Bruce stocked enough food for an army. Don't know when I'll have the chance to call again, but Loretta has all the numbers for Zeno if you can't reach Catherine."

"Do you have any idea where Sam and Tekla are? If they're injured?"

"We think they survived the plane's emergency landing and are in someone's custody. We're assuming the government but can't rule out *La Bière*. We're on it. Keep the faith, Mrs. Webster."

"I've got faith, Mr. Webster, it's patience that trips me up."

"Slammed by truth?" Maggie repeated as she studied Jacques and Catherine—brilliant, flawed, human rights warriors. For the past decade, she'd imbued them with mystical powers for her salvation—the *exposé* one wingbeat away until it wasn't.

After a lifetime of labored attempts through the lava, ashes, and soot of her many-fabricated selves, Maggie cleared her throat and unleashed a force so deep, so distant, it silenced fear. "Right now, I don't give a flying fuck about who I am, who you are, or how we ended up in this godawful place. Sam and Tekla are missing. That is the only truth. I want you to quit treating me like a candy-ass and put me to work."

# 14

# The Press Release

WEDNESDAY, SEPTEMBER 21, 1977—*Early yesterday, two Americans were abducted following a mayday emergency landing or plane crash—all within clear view of the Maple Airport near Toronto, Canada. Not random Americans, but the thirty-two-year-old son-in-law and eight-year-old granddaughter of Raymond and Anna Soulier, Canada's two most notorious French-Canadian secessionists who disappeared twenty-seven years ago without a trace.*

*Almost twenty-four hours have passed and still no press—no public outcry, no known activity by the Civil Aviation Directorate, Mounties, or intelligence agencies in Canada or the United States.*

*Today, Oz, an international human rights group, initiated a search to find Sam Tervo and his daughter, Tekla Moonwalker Tervo. Mr. Tervo and his daughter were last seen leaving the landing or crash site in a black van. . .*

*Oz will provide copies of all known documents—collected or created by Raymond and Anna Soulier—to Canadian and U.S.*

*authorities; media packets will be delivered to major newspapers and television news' stations. . .*

*Oz invites anyone who has information that might lead to the safe return of Sam and Tekla to contact Oz representatives at Zeno Development by calling . . .*

"Reward or no reward?" asked Catherine.

Maggie lifted her shoulders, palms up. "Help me here—pros, cons?"

"Mixed. The number of unreliable sightings increases a hundredfold when there's a reward and it costs time. The upside is a reward gets more banter, more local talk at the corner grocery. Even a casual sighting of an eight-year-old girl with three grown men would strike a chord."

"I'm for striking all the chords we can."

"Let's do it. Add a five-thousand-dollar reward for information leading to their safe return."

Maggie typed the final line of the press release and pulled it out of Jacques' old Underwood typewriter. After Catherine's review, she handed it to Bernadette, who was called away from the assembly line to manage the document library and provide third-floor clerical support.

By the time Bruce walked into Zeno's lobby at 8:00 a.m., the noise level was a drum-brush scat of gathering decibels. Conference tables around the perimeter of the first floor served as an assembly-line for the production and distribution of media packets. Carla, on the loading dock in the back, directed dolly traffic from Toronto's three largest printing companies—signing and filing bills of lading. Clyde, in charge of security, managed the guards, reviewed questionable press IDs, and ensured Canadian and U.S. intelligence agency officials were immediately escorted to the third floor.

Emma, as always, 'owned' the reception area with her non-flappable, pragmatic charm. Long waits seemed short with food carts offering fresh coffee, almond croissants, and chocolate pralines. Despite the potential for hectic or festive energy, the tone was focused and productive. Everyone understood the reputation and integrity of at least two free nations were on the line. Poster-board photos of Sam and Tekla, displayed on easels throughout the lobby, discouraged any temptation to downplay the gravity or urgency of their work.

When Bruce bounded into the third-floor office area, the last person he expected to see was Maggie—her cat eyes greener and more almond-shaped than an Abyssinian. He stood still.

"Bruce Shelton, we meet again."

"Maggie, I can only imagine how angry, confused and betrayed you must feel."

"Don't flatter yourself, and don't expect me to soothe your tender feelings. You're nothing to me. This is not about you, or me. This is about Sam and Tekla.

"Here's how we're set up. You, Catherine and Jacques, will share Jacques' office. Catherine's office is the swing office—slash—interview room. The conference room is set up for meetings of four to eight. Clyde's the point person for prioritizing and scheduling meetings. We're on the job twenty-four-seven. Sandwiches in paper bags and beverages will be available throughout the day and night. Any questions?"

"Little Sister, please understand. We never meant to hurt you or anyone. It was all about protecting you from yourself. Giving you a wake-up call. We underestimated the dark-side."

"Tell me, whose dark side?"

By four o'clock, the conference rooms on the first and third floors held detectives and agents; the cafeteria hosted reporters from major network lions to suburban weekly cubs. Maggie, Carla and Bernadette huddled in the copy room/breakroom on the second floor to stoke the flow of paper, mail and hotline calls.

From the lobby, Emma's switchboard was set up to receive and forward hotline calls to Clyde, Bernadette or Carla.

"Reward Hotline, may I help you?" said Emma.

"Is this Emma?"

"This is Emma. Who's speaking?"

"Emma, this is Sam Tervo. Jacques' private line was busy. Tekla's here with me. We're alone, we're okay. I need you to keep this line open and get Jacques. I'm short on quarters. Take down this number if we get disconnected . . ."

"Got it! I'm off. Don't move!"

Emma's black, blunt-cut hair spun like a whirlybird as she ran head-first up four half-flights of stairs, two steps at a time. By the third landing, the hush in the lobby was so complete it seemed to crave sensation.

Two minutes later Emma flew down the stairs, hurdled over her desk, and picked up the receiver. Eighteen people watched her whisper into the phone and transfer the call.

Maggie didn't need to look up. She felt Catherine's energy move the air like a promise before she heard her whisper, "Sam and Tekla are okay. Come upstairs. They're on the phone."

Gripping the edge of the typewriter stand, Maggie twisted sideways and saw the rush of certainty and relief in Catherine's eyes. She almost knocked Catherine down—getting up and out of the door—before she dashed up the stairs to Jacques' office.

"Hold on Sam, Maggie just walked in."

"Sam? Where are . . ."

Jacques got in Maggie's face and shook his head.

"Forget that. More important, how are you and Tekla?"

“We’re good. We’ve been on the craziest scavenger hunt for the past few days. I’m not sure Tekla was all that thrilled with it. I talked her into leaving Windsor Dog at home, which turned out to be a bad idea. Let me put her on the phone.”

“Hey, Moonwalker, I’ve missed you!”

“Where are you?”

“I’m here in Toronto with Jacques and Catherine. We’ve been looking for you. What kind of scavenger hunt have you been on?”

Maggie could hear Tekla taking deep breaths, she was crying.

“I’m not a baby . . . the plane almost . . . almost crashed . . . in a field. There was a fire truck.” With each gasp of air, Maggie knew Tekla was fighting back tears and tapping her left foot with self-impatience.

“It’s okay, Moonwalker, you can tell me.”

“It’s NOT okay. There was NO stupid scavenger hunt. Sam made that up so I wouldn’t be afraid. I just want to go home.”

“I know, my brave girl. Me too.”

# 15

# Collateral Damage

THURSDAY MORNING, SEPTEMBER 22, 1977—Maggie rolled over. She wanted to nuzzle Tekla's neck and kiss her on the cheek, but both she and Sam appeared to be deep in REM sleep. It was almost midnight when they finally arrived at Zeno, a place everyone thought offered the best protection from paparazzi and more serious threats. Catherine had arranged a move from Maggie's small room to one twice the size, with a sitting area, kitchenette, and two double beds. Emma made runs for fresh clothes and toiletries. And Jacque's long-time chef, Charles, moved into Maggie's old room and opened Zeno's cafeteria to prepare hamburgers, French fries, and coleslaw. Tekla's "most favorite."

Last night, hungry, spent, and awed, Maggie watched their homecoming meal play out like a silent movie. Other than occasional whispered words, heads nodded, shoulders shrugged, fingers touched, and lips smiled as warmth circled the table—she, Sam, Tekla, Jacques, Catherine, Clyde, Blanche, and Loretta leaning in toward one other. The wrecking crew and Bruce weren't there. They stayed at Marc's *pensione,* the Maple Leaf. Maggie still couldn't wrap her head around that scene. When she and Sam first visited the Maple Leaf in 1968, she'd convinced herself that Marc was a Neanderthal and bigot. Now he appeared to be part of the 'Oz family,' a low-life thug hiding under a prayer veil. *Like Bruce? Like everyone at Oz?*

Maggie slipped off her side of the bed, straightened the covers, and took in the familiar, musty scents. What in god's name possessed her to think she wanted something else, something more? Why would she risk her family for anyone or anything else? Her mother did, and Maggie's attempt to rewrite her mother's memoir had already cost twenty years. But no more flipping reality in search of fantasy. Maggie was determined her time with Jacques, Catherine and Oz would be over as soon as they could make the break.

The second double bed held new clothes for each of them. Maggie pulled on a pair of bell-bottom jeans, a mustard-colored turtleneck and slipped into a pair of black clogs. Leaving a note on the table for Sam and Tekla to meet her for coffee and croissants on the third floor, Maggie took one last look before she gently closed the door and wondered if she'd ever feel safe again.

Last night, before Sam and Tekla arrived, Catherine announced that almost every major newspaper in North America was carrying Oz's story. And with every new exposé and each reporter's interpretation of the facts, Catherine warned us to expect the lines to be blurred—between right and wrong, good and bad, moral and immoral. Conspiracy theorists had already generated headlines to capture shoppers at grocery store check-out lines; one claimed Sam master-minded the plane crash and kidnapped Tekla to secure a ransom large enough to pay his gambling debts.

For the US and Canada, the stakes were higher, the issues more complex. Globally, the tension raised by the confidential reports—implicating intelligence agencies, judges, watchdog groups—threatened security across the planet. The name Oz no longer brought up images of a whimsical, fictional place. Now, Oz insinuated a force strong enough to tip the balance of power on this rotating sphere we call home.

Plagued by this report—and an anthology of unhinged conspiracy theories tugging at her imagination—Maggie wondered if Oz's silence about the juicers' use of DEPC, to preserve fruit drinks and poison people, was intended to up the ante. How do the world's intelligence agencies line up on the issues of corruption, capitalism and power? Does any country or international organization have the force, power, money—or, god forbid, will—to upend a lucrative industry, a famous brewery?

Sunrise was filtering through the window in the anteroom when Catherine sat down next to Maggie, poured herself a coffee and said, "Tell me, did the three of you just crash?"

Maggie smiled and nodded her head. Last night, their synchronized backward flop on the bed, clothes and all, took what little energy they had. The time between sliding under the covers and grunting goodnight was lost in fatigue, gratitude, and sweet sleep. "Yes. We crashed in the best possible way. How about you?"

"I think we both fell asleep with smiles on our faces. I can't imagine how we could have survived days of not knowing."

"You didn't know?"

"We didn't know. Maggie, you have the right to question everything and I hope you do. We knew Clyde and Sam planned the trip to make sure you were okay. Oz hired the first pilot. The mechanical problem was no doubt set up by *La Bière* to delay the flight and swap in their pilot. *La Bière* may have gotten word when you crossed the border; but, when you asked for copies of their business records two days later, the alarms detonated. Based on what little Sam was able to say in front of Tekla, it sounds like all bets were off after the pilot and van driver got to know her. They both have kids."

"And me? Why kidnap me? Couldn't you have rescued me?"

"When Bruce discovered the two security guys had been shot, there was no time. We had to get you away without debate. The helicopter was ready to lift off in minutes. The twilight sleep sedation made you feel like you were moving in slow motion, forgetting things, losing touch—but you made it here in record time."

Maggie shook her head and looked down. How many years had she wasted trying to find her parents? Hoping that Catherine was Anna? That Jacques was her real father? Why in god's name would she want parents who ignored her lifelong angst, let corporations poison children, and treat her like an enemy? Something must be radically wrong with her. Here she was, once again, feeling grateful not to be locked in a room. *Talk about the Stockholm Effect,* she thought, *I'm the poster child—ready to commit my husband and child to the same abuse.*

"Maggie are you okay?" asked Catherine.

"Sorry, just lost in reverie about finding Sam and Tekla. I left a note for them to meet me here after they wake up. We'll be leaving as soon as we can."

Catherine reached out to touch Maggie's hand and saw her flinch. Lowering her voice, she said, "I can only imagine how eager you are to be home, to find the normal. If Jacques and I have any regrets, it's waiting this long to bring you into the fold. There's no way to change that. We'll all pay for this mistake. But hear me. We need time to debrief. You and Sam are the key targets—there's so much you'll want to know before you get caught in the media blitz. And Tekla . . . she needs to hear the news from you, not her schoolmates."

Maggie felt trapped between her fight or flight responses. She turned sideways and looked at Catherine. There was something familiar—old, remote, but, without question, familiar. Yet, unable to connect her thoughts to her feelings, Maggie felt agitated. "What do we need to know?"

"We sent out volumes of information. Most of it relates to Oz and the underground money changers, empire builders. But, my love, there's information about you and your family that you'll want to know. We can begin debriefing today, but I think it will take days, if not weeks, before you and Sam work out a plan for yourselves—where you want to live and who you want to invite into your lives."

Maggie bowed her head and thought about the huge packets of information they'd shipped to newspapers across the continent. For her, the goal was limited to finding Sam and Tekla. Even if she'd had time to look at the documents, Maggie had no reason to believe the information affected her or Sam.

"Maggie, I know you want to get home. But hear me out. Emma's heading this way with her two daughters and a trunkload of puzzles, books and board games. There's no doubt Tekla needs some light, ordinary re-entry time. Charles is setting up the cafeteria for a play day and intends to help the girls plan and prepare lunch. We can get started on the debrief."

"Tomorrow, then. We'll head home tomorrow," said Maggie.

"I'm ready!" called Sam, as he peeked inside the door.

"Me, too!" cried Tekla, as she wriggled between Sam and the door jam. "Windsor Dog misses me. He doesn't like it when I'm gone."

Maggie grabbed Tekla by her waist and turned her around. "Goodness, gracious, great balls of fire, are these clean clothes and mud-free tennies?"

Tekla looked down at her new clothes and tugged at her tee shirt, whispering, "I don't think Uncle Willie would like me in a Maple Leaf jersey."

"Nope, you're right about that. Might not play so well in Detroit."

Tekla's laugh sounded like a prophecy.

# 16

# The Exposé

THURSDAY, MID-MORNING, SEPTEMBER 22, 1977—Tucked away on the third floor, behind Jacques and Catherine's suite of offices, the small metal door led to the most captivating secret-space Maggie had ever encountered. On the east, floor to ceiling windows framed Lake Ontario, importing light, texture, and marine commerce to the warehouse-sized room. The battered hardwood floor provided contrast to the lines, arcs and circles of moveable cabinets, tables, and chairs. Along the west wall, the remnants of a ship's galley with chicken-wired cupboard doors, and a tung-lacquered driftwood bar, invited foraging. *A companion room to the cafeteria where she and Sam first met Jacques in August 1968,* thought Maggie. More than nine years of unexplained, bizarre, dangerous encounters that led to this gathering with maybe friends, maybe relatives, and the certainty of her incident-based paranoia.

Although Maggie knew she was on solid ground, the floor felt as if it was loosely moored to a pier and lifted by the tide. Sam grabbed her hand and led her to the small circle of curved-back chairs and turned toward her.

"Maggie, listen to me. We have no idea what we're about to hear or how this might change our lives. But, for Tekla's sake, our sake, we've got to pay attention. We don't have to make our peace here. Later, we'll talk—take all the time we need—before we decide what we want to do. You okay?"

Maggie looked at Sam with new eyes; like her, like everyone, he too was flawed, broken, strong, smart, thick-headed. Somehow, without conflict, Maggie finally grokked the importance of being both charmed and chagrined by her mate. Her walk across floes of ice to find perfection with Bruce had been a disaster; her romance with synchronicity short-lived. Other than a belief in magical thinking, or a concierge god, Maggie wondered why any sane adult would think perfection was some objective, static phenom—or that synchronicity meant nirvana. She, a thirty-something mother looking for a 'daddy' found Bruce; he, a middle-aged man with his own set of demons had an empty bed. Amen.

Leaning over, Sam whispered, "Hey, Mag, where are you? You okay?"

Maggie nodded, then looked around the room. Jacques, Catherine, Clyde, Blanche, Loretta—last night's dinner guests—were gathering, choosing their seats. All Oz. No Bruce. Two chairs too many.

Loretta sat on Maggie's right, put her arm over her shoulder and whispered in her ear, "Hey, baby, I know you're freaked, but you've been waiting a long time for this day. I'm here for you, no one else. You need anything, I'll do it."

Maggie looked at Loretta and ran through the memories they'd made, shared, dissected and rewrote; reels of tapes imprinting their friendship and mapping their lives. Reels, like those she shared with Clyde and Blanche, who took seats next to Loretta, as if filling out Maggie's team bench. Jacques and Catherine had settled into chairs facing her and Sam. Two chairs remained empty.

Catherine looked up, nodded and said, "Thanks for being here—for your friendship and support. Our gathering might have seemed hasty, unplanned, but Jacques and I have imagined this day for decades. In candor, imagined and dreaded this day. Now that it's here, we find ourselves relieved, almost manic, to expose secrets we've dragged around far too long, at a cost to everyone in this room and . . ." Catherine closed her eyes and took two deep breaths before she continued, ". . . and to millions of people who might have enjoyed a longer and healthier life if we hadn't kept this information to ourselves. We have many regrets and we're prepared for the recriminations we deserve. You do not. Yet, you will be targeted, your lives undeniably stressed by the burden we've placed on you. For this, there is not enough time or money to make up for our wrong thinking, but we'll do our best.

"Any sense of relief we feel by unloading the truth does not diminish or absolve our decision to deceive, and likely hurt, the people we love. We twisted reality and imposed fiction on our family and friends. Most appallingly—criminally—we didn't blow the whistle on the juicers. For what? Did we think hoarding power would lead to a better world? Think of it. Cancer centers were adding rooms, pediatric suites, children's wards. How many men, women and children suffered and died while we jousted for power?

"Three days ago, when we heard about Sam and Tekla's plane crash and disappearance, we stopped imagining power and acted on it. We papered the world with truth—purging ourselves of a lifetime of lies and releasing a weapon we hoped was powerful enough to gain their safe return.

"Each of you has paid the price for these lies—your time, energy, love and support for one another. And the many unexplained crises necessary to feed this alternate reality."

Maggie uncrossed her legs and planted both feet on the floor. The illusory tide had seceded with these words. The quiet stillness seemed a welcome breath, a yogi's pose. When Maggie looked up, everyone's head was down, as if the moment and message deserved this prayerful countenance. When Sam lifted her hand and raised it to his cheek, she felt his first tear, then her own. Despite her reckless, lifelong search for the cold, hard truth—Maggie knew her tears weren't about relief. Pulling her hand away from Sam, Maggie was desperate to shift gears. The yogi's pose was beginning to piss her off. She wanted to get a bag of chips and a Coke from the galley—engage in small talk, maintain the status quo.

For a few moments, Catherine watched Maggie's agitation as she looked for an exit, a way out, then said, "Let's step back and cover some housekeeping items. The small bar is open all day. You'll find healthy and not-so-healthy snacks, coffee, tea, soda pop. We'll exercise adult freedoms and ask that you help yourselves. The entire building is locked and access to the third floor has been closed off because Tekla and her two new friends are busy helping Charles in the cafeteria. The loo near the elevator is open. If you need access to another floor—or anything else—let me know.

"Today, we'll do what we can to summarize decades of misinformation and covert decisions. Whether it affects you directly or indirectly, it's essential you know what we unleashed on suspecting intelligence agencies and the unsuspecting public. No doubt we'll get sued and pilloried by the press. If you're personally sued or pilloried, we want to know. We'll cover any legal costs and attempt to counter the wrath of scandal sheets and gossip columns.

"When we made the decision to release Anna and Raymond's documents, we did it with our eyes, hearts and minds wide open. Some of you know about their work with Oz, but few of you know the extent and impact of their research. The short story is we decided to yank the corporate veil off corruption and expose Oz's playbook. On a more personal, more invisible front, this same information has the muscle to keep us together or tear us apart. Today we'll focus on the more personal, invisible front, and ask each of you to listen, ask questions, offer opinions, cast doubt, and challenge our thinking. This is the place to do it because we need one another to support Oz's work and protect every scrap of personal privacy that comes our way. Jacques?"

Jacques rolled his shoulders back, tucked his chin down, then looked at Maggie. "I can't imagine how this information is hitting you or how hard it might be to process. There's no way to explain all the subtleties, words, thoughts, circumstances that led us here. Thirty-some years ago Oz was a group of young, inexperienced revolutionaries seduced by a sense of purpose. Our comrades in Oz's peaceful resistance, Raymond and Anna, burned hot. They ignited our work and our souls. With each firestorm lit by Anna's words, the resistance took on grit and Oz began to threaten the world's power brokers. Huh. At times we scared ourselves with our perceived power and began to back away.

"To reduce the chance of defectors, we reinvented Oz. We built walls between members, first names only; then messed around with meeting times. Nothing we did was predictable. It seemed the perfect foil. Emboldened, Anna's attacks on the establishment became more personal and brutal. Unsettled, Raymond's growing anxiety worsened." Jacques paused, looked down, and rubbed his hands together. Clearing his throat, he continued, "Hmm. To be clear, Raymond was bright, wickedly funny, and kind. Yet, there were times when Raymond jumped the rails and acted completely insane. When those times became more frequent, it was clear he posed a threat to Oz, Anna's work . . . and to Anna herself.

"Their 1950 trip along the St. Lawrence Seaway was designed to help them find the space, cover, and medical support they'd need to continue their work. At the time, we had a few safe houses along the Seaway and one in Nova Scotia. No one at Oz, including me, expected them to vanish. And for years, no one knew where they were." Jacques looked at Catherine and she nodded.

Clearing his throat again, Jacques began in a voice so soft Maggie leaned forward to hear him. "Catherine and I decided I'd take this thread of the story because it's easier to tell from my perspective. Huh, maybe not so easy." Jacques cleared his throat, then continued, "You see, just before Christmas in 1959, I received a call . . . um . . . late in the day, after dark. I was measuring space in this building, planning to make the leap from a storefront to a warehouse. A woman's voice, she said she just got off the train at Union Station and needed a lift. Before I could respond, she whispered, 'Look for a redhead with a purple scarf' and hung up.

"Black ice and snow had turned Toronto into a skating rink, but I was prepared to skate if I had to. I was in a state of wonder. Anna!"

# 17

# The Great Deceit

THURSDAY MID-MORNING, SEPTEMBER 22, 1977—Anna's name toppled the meeting. Eyes widened; jaws dropped. Maggie was literally on the edge of her seat. Moving to the edge of her chair, Catherine looked at Maggie and said, "I, too, can't conceive how difficult this might be for you. When Jacques and I talked about how we wanted to tell our story we—rightly or wrongly—decided our telling deserved time and enough detail to cover the sights, sounds, and feelings that accompany the words. We also wanted you to be surrounded by friends." Turning her attention to the group, Catherine saw concern and empathy in their eyes and body language. Both she and Jacques had hoped their presence would cushion the blows and ease Maggie's transition to the truth.

Maggie cleared her throat, held her hand up, and said, "One question before Jacques continues his story about my mother. Who, besides me, is hearing this for the first time?"

Blanche, Sam and Loretta raised their hands.

Maggie looked at Clyde and whispered, "You knew?"

"Just this week. Once the decision was made to paper the world, I was assigned the media. I had to know what was out there . . . but for all these years, Maggie, I didn't know."

Sliding back in her chair, Maggie said, "Okay, I'm ready. Let's hear more about Anna, the orphan-maker." Maggie heard Sam whisper "ouch," and she was glad to know her response stung—until she saw Catherine's bowed head and rounded shoulders.

Jacques leaned forward, elbow on knee, chin on fist, as if testing his will to continue, then said, "In candor, Catherine and I may have been too hasty—or, more likely—overthought the importance of taking our time. Perhaps she and I are the only ones who need a slower pace to reconstruct the early days. If you're willing, Maggie, I'd like to go slow this morning and see how it works. If it turns out to be tedious, we'll speed things up this afternoon. Agreed?"

Everyone understood that Maggie's sharp-nod, tight-lipped agreement was no olive branch. Loretta knew Maggie was running on fumes. Just months after Janis Joplin died, Maggie announced she'd adopted Joplin's version of *Me and Bobby McGee* as her personal anthem. Loretta could almost hear Maggie belting out 'freedom's just another word for nothing left to lose.' Could almost see her taking over the stage at some Austin dive—stoned out of her mind, her voice like gravel—tossing words and mic stands to tempt the gods.

Jacques' slow, solemn nod seemed to acknowledge the prickly codicils contained in Maggie's nod. Sitting up straight, he said, "Back to Anna. My state of wonder was tested as soon as my new 1959 Peugeot hit a patch of black ice and spun counter-clockwise; a breathtaking three-sixty on a narrow city street without a dent. I was holding on to the sound of Anna's voice—her every word. Only a few blocks away, she was waiting for me. Downshifting to second gear, I slowed the car, but not my racing heart.

"If you haven't been there, Union Station dominates Front Street with twenty-two gigantic limestone columns. Filthy from decades of coal use, this Beaux-Arts paragon is still Toronto's grand dame. Inside the barrel-vaulted Great Hall—about the size of an NHL hockey rink—travelers move from one impressive arched window to another. Soaring eighty-eight feet high, Missouri stone walls hold curved ceilings of carved stone and Guastavino tile. At its base, a herringbone pattern of Tennessee marble jazzes up tired floors. Not as opulent as Detroit's Fisher Theatre, with its spectacular barrel-vaulted lobby flashing forty different kinds of marble. Yet, both buildings evoke awe, almost reverence, for the sheer magnitude of the undertaking and the acres of exquisite detail. All the back-breaking, untold hours of work by artists, craftsmen, stonemasons and laborers." Jacques took a sip of cold coffee and scanned the room before saying, "Sorry. I'm sure I'm driving you nuts rattling on and on about cars and architecture. My modus operandi—these convenient distractions and diversions, head stuff. You see . . . what I'm about to tell you still brings me to my knees. Here goes.

"That night the Great Hall was nearly deserted. A small woman in a black coat with a purple babushka edged out of the shadows. Hunched over, she was limping and dragging her left foot. Her black lace-up shoes were those of an old woman or nun. I was about to look away when she tugged the bottom of her left sleeve. Huh . . . back in the forties . . . it was one of the signals Anna insisted Oz adopt after a long day of conspiracy theory busting and too much wine."

Jacques paused and looked at Catherine, then Maggie. Maggie's left knee was jumping up and down in time with Jacques' left knee. He crossed his legs, right over left, took a deep breath, then continued.

"Trapped in disbelief, I couldn't move. I watched this old woman tip her head forward, crank her arms, and drag her left foot, as if she was determined to reach me before I reached her." Jacques looked down and pumped his shoulders three times before tears came.

Sam squeezed Maggie's hand. She leaned her head on his shoulder and whispered, "Please, no more disappearing."

After Jacques cleared his throat, he said, "There was such grace in that moment. One of those times when we get knocked over by beauty . . . love . . . or courage. Sometimes all three.

"When the woman reached me, she smiled with her eyes, then her mouth. I wanted to believe it was Anna, but not this old, crippled, toothless bag lady. Her top four incisors were missing, and her cheeks deeply hollowed. A mean-looking keloid scar stretched from the corner of her left eye to her left earlobe, pulling up the left side of her mouth in a sneer. It was clear she hadn't . . .um . . . received medical attention." Jacques dropped his head and paused a long time before Catherine took his hand.

Placing his other hand over hers, Jacques said, "The shadow woman's black wool coat and purple scarf looked clean, but the stench of unwashed skin and hair told another story. At some disturbing, visceral level, I wanted to shun this old woman. It had to be a trap. But she had these amazing, intelligent eyes—deep green with flecks of gold. I'd lost myself in these eyes before. Afraid to hug her broken body, I touched her shoulders and said, 'My god, Anna, where have you been? Who did this to you?'

"And this, dear friends . . . this was the beginning of the great deceit."

Maggie turned sideways and held onto the back of her chair to stand up. Her entire body was shaking. She knew she and Jacques were at the precipice. For almost a decade he'd been her ghost partner, acting out a scene that had been way over-rehearsed and in danger of being cut from the script. When Sam and Tekla went missing, Maggie thought she stopped caring about anything else, especially her long-lost parents. She was wrong. Right now, Maggie didn't give a rip if Jacques and Catherine recoiled at her intended outburst. Seizing the moment and pointing her finger at Jacques, Maggie's voice broke in loud bits.

"Screw this! . . . It might be . . . might be . . . your great deceit, but you're talking about Anna . . . my mother. You can justify your actions on your own time . . . write a memoir or novel. I don't give a rip." Maggie bent over, then stood up and took a deep breath. This time, there was no ice-cold clarity and calm to rescue her from the abyss. Still shaking, Maggie forced herself to turn down her volume and mimic self-confidence as she said, "If you somehow convinced yourself that you're protecting me, get a life. I don't want or need your protection or confinement or whatever the hell you call it. What I want from you is the answer to three questions. One—what did you do to protect my mother? Two—where has she been for the past twenty-seven years? And three—where is she right now?"

# 18

# Gauntlets

THURSDAY MID-DAY, SEPTEMBER 22, 1977—Maggie's intrepid gauntlet filled the room.

Surprised by his temptation to stand and scold this impetuous young woman, Jacques sat back, held his hands in a prayer position against his lips and watched Maggie resettle in her chair. Her impatience to uncover the truth was way overdue. But his left and right brain wanted to rumble. For him and Catherine the challenge was navigating decades of facts and feelings held hostage by secrets and promises. Their decision to exploit this information to secure Sam and Tekla's release made sense. *But,* thought Jacques, *why, in the name of all deities, did we decide on a support group? Was it for Maggie's sake? Or did Catherine and I convene this charade as our shield?*

Catherine touched Jacques' shoulder and said, "I'll take it from here. You see, Jacques and I made the decision to paper the world with this story. We thought it was the only way to free Sam and Tekla. Most of these documents reveal crimes committed by respected politicians, manufacturers, lawyers, judges, intelligence agents—with or without the help of not-so-respected mobsters. There's no doubt we're surrounded by a syndicate of powerful enemies. But, in some perverse way, these same papers offer Oz and each person in this room a whistleblower-kind of protection.

"In addition to blowing the whistle we broke long-held promises and revealed personal secrets. Revelations capable of ripping families apart and threatening memories that define who we were . . . and perhaps . . . who we are.

"My dear Maggie, Jacques and I watched and listened. We knew how determined you were to solve the disappearance of Raymond and Anna. We also knew there was no way you could fathom the number of tripwires attached to this mystery. As each year passed, disclosing the truth seemed riskier and less important. Jacques and I thought we could divert your attention—keep you safe, keep the lies safe, continue our shadow connections. We were wrong.

"So here we are with only a few days to unpack the secrets and promises. To do this we need the secret-holders and promise-givers in the room. After almost three decades of looking for answers, we understand your impatience and frustration. But, for all that time, the secret-holders—including Jacques and me—were just as determined to hide the answers.

"Now that these documents are public, you and Sam will want this information to protect yourselves and Tekla. These two empty chairs will soon be occupied and most of your questions will be answered—if not today, then tomorrow. Will you stay another day?"

"The truth? Huh. I wonder if I'll recognize it. I'm okay with another day if Sam's on board. But that's it; no more."

Catherine looked at Sam and he nodded yes. "Okay, then. Jacques and I will ramp this up and let the other two guests know when to arrive. Any questions?"

Maggie lifted her index finger and said, "Is there some reason you're not giving us the names of these two . . . um . . . guests?"

"You're right; this isn't a tea party. In answer to your question, we haven't given you their names because we want you to know the context first. Our thinking was . . . is, if we give you their names before we give you the backstories, you'll be tempted to revisit every conversation you had with them and miss important details about who or what influenced the secrets and promises. I'm sure this sounds convoluted and codependent as hell."

Subtle nods and grimaces punctuated Maggie's thinking before she said, "No, it's okay. I get it."

Looking at her watch, Catherine said, "Let's break for lunch—thirty minutes to eat, stretch, and visit the loo. Jacques and I have a few calls to make."

Instead of the usual paper-bag sandwiches, Charles delivered two iron skillets filled with quiche and a driftwood tray of salad greens. After setting out plates, napkins, and silverware, he opened a tabletop easel to display a handwritten chalkboard message:

TODAY'S MENU

Quiche Lorraine

Romaine Hearts, Dressed in Caesar

Sprinkled with fresh parmesan + peppercorns.

Bon Appetite!

Master Chefs: Tekla, Sarah + Danielle

Loretta wheeled two chairs to the windowed wall where Maggie was standing and said, "Hey, baby, you okay?"

Pulled away from the harbor view—where people were working, doing their own thing, living their lives—Maggie shook her head and said, "I have no idea how I'm doing. One minute I'm jumping out of my skin because I feel trapped by the lies and cloak and dagger threats. The next minute, I think, finally, this is it! Before I finish that thought, all kinds of alarms go off. Before Sam and Tekla went missing, I could handle the madness. Not now. Now I'm beginning to feel like Sam, Tekla and I are the prey."

"Here's what I know," said Loretta, "Jacques and Catherine are for real—they're the good guys. When they gave up Anna's documents, they risked their lives and the future of Oz to safeguard Sam and Tekla. Before they released the documents, you were right to worry. The threats were real. I'm not saying you're home free, but you're damn close. It's too late for the bad guys to bury the truth."

Before Maggie had a chance to consider her reply, Blanche walked up with two plates of food and handed one to Maggie and the other to Loretta and said, "Time to eat."

"Grab a chair and join us," said Loretta.

Blanche looked at Maggie; Maggie smiled and said, "Of course, yes! Get your plate and sit with us."

Sam and Clyde were in deep conversation at the bar. There was no sign of Jacques or Catherine.

After Blanche pulled up her chair, Maggie whispered, "Do either of you know the mystery people?"

Blanche shook her head no.

Loretta scanned the room and whispered, "I don't think we need to whisper," then laughed at herself and spoke up. "Seriously, I have no idea who they are, but I hope one of them is Anna. What about you? Any hopes?"

"Nope. None. I'm tired of hoping. For too long I convinced myself that Catherine was Anna. The story about Anna's disfigured face almost caused me to pick up that torch again. But no. When I look at Catherine, there's not any . . . you know . . . psychic pull," said Maggie.

"Not sure psychic pull works when you're stressed to the max," said Loretta.

Blanche nodded and said, "You've been whacked big time. I can't imagine how hard it is to stay calm. Okay. You're probably not calm. Are you?"

Maggie opened her eyes as wide as she could and mocked a silent scream.

"Guess not!" laughed Loretta.

Jumping up, Blanche said, "Enough sitting. We need to get some blood flowing! I know, we can do our impression of The Supremes singing . . . what?"

"How about *Stop in the Name of Love?*" said Maggie, "Pun intended!"

Loretta jumped up, spun Maggie's chair and said, "Let's do it! We need—what's it called—a humor break? No, close but . . ."

"Comic relief?" offered Blanche.

"That's it! We're desperate for comic relief."

And before they had time to think about it, they were shaking their hips, extending their right arms straight out, hands flat up, singing, "Stop in the name of love, before you break my heart . . .Think it o—o—ver!" When they missed words, or skipped entire stanzas, they hummed or started over. It didn't matter.

Sam and Clyde whistled and clapped as 'The Supremes' took deep, dramatic bows.

Out of breath, grinning from ear-to-ear, Loretta, Blanche and Maggie huddled. Before anyone spoke, Blanche squinted her eyes and gave Maggie her 'no-bullshit-look'—the one she perfected after the birth of her third son. Then, she snapped her fingers with a sharp arc to the right. Whether you knew Blanche or not, anyone in close range of her snap knew this meant *listen up!* In a voice that commanded attention, Blanche said, "Marguerite Soulier Tervo, you've been waiting for this day a long time. Whatever comes up, whatever happens, we're here for you. But, make no mistake, you

WILL listen. After that, we'll help you kick ass, give you alone time, plan a family reunion, whatever you need. You hear me?"

Maggie leaned against Blanche's shoulder and whispered, "I hear you and I thank you."

The sound of the metal door opening turned their heads. Catherine walked in and invited everyone to move their chairs back in a circle. By the time Jacques walked in, everyone was sitting, waiting.

Nodding at Catherine, Jacques sat down and, with his signature grace, made silent contact with each person before he said, "I thought you'd like to know that I met with the Master Chefs and thanked them for the wonderful quiche and salad. Right now, they're planning dessert for our afternoon coffee break. On my way out, Tekla tugged my sleeve and confided it would be okay if we left tips."

Sam smiled and said, "Who else?"

"Ah! She's got Maggie's pluck," laughed Loretta.

"That she does," said Jacques.

"Before we move on," Jacques continued, "are there any questions from this morning? . . . Nothing? . . . Okay, then, some announcements. I spoke to the two unnamed people and we're set to meet with them this evening or tomorrow morning. Scheduling will depend on time, energy and emotional fitness. Maggie and Sam will make those calls. As for the girls, Emma and Charles have worked out a plan for a pajama party if we run late.

"No matter how we cut it, this is going to be one long day. Once we give you the context, I think you'll understand why this on-ramp piece is important. I'll start.

"The backstory begins in 1944. Canada, like most of the free world, was supplying soldiers, doctors, nurses, money, and provisions to halt the Nazis and other Axis belligerents. Almost one million Canadian men volunteered for duty. And our Canadian women rolled up their sleeves and put on bandanas—replacing men in factories; working the farms; running the shops; driving trucks, buses and trains. They built ships, tested munitions and kept the home fires burning.

"On June 6, 1944, D-Day, British, American and Canadian forces landed on the beaches of Normandy. Those who survived continued fighting the Third Reich across France and into Germany. And here, on Canadian shores, German U-boats invaded the St. Lawrence River and Gulf of St. Lawrence. German subs, with newly designed snorkels, were skulking off the Atlantic shores of Canada and Nova Scotia.

"Most Canadians felt unsafe, many for the first time in their lives. Canadian women, who found themselves pregnant and unmarried, suffered the most. Society was willing to accept women who repaired artillery tanks in war zones and built bombers in factories at home; but god forbid, society did not accept women who had sex before marriage. Toward the end of the war, the number of unwed mothers was breaking records in allied and axis countries. In Canada, forced adoptions of 'illegitimate' newborns were legally permitted and encouraged by the government. For Catholic women everywhere, sex without marriage was a mortal sin.

"This socially-unacceptable—most grievous sin—darkened lives, destroyed families and, too often, led to back-alley abortions or suicides. Women were second-class citizens; unmarried pregnant women had almost no rights. Two generations later, we're here to unravel the truth. Catherine, are you ready?"

# 19

# No Flash Cards

THURSDAY AFTERNOON, SEPTEMBER 22, 1977—Catherine exhaled as if she'd been holding her breath. "I thought I could take this on without the foreboding of those days, but that's not going to happen . . . so . . . hmm . . . please be patient if I wander a bit.

"On May 8, 1945—Victory in Europe or VE Day—I was a twenty-six-year-old wife and mother. Married to the radical activist I met when Oz was organizing Canada in the Thirties, we were two of a kind when it came to music, politics, and social justice. He was the 'fire-starter;' I was the writer. This smart, crazy, good-looking, romantic man chose me! At first it felt like luck. Later, his craziness began to seize control of our lives. As if wired for sound, he'd pace the floor, shout profanities at good-for-nothing-gods, then disappear for days. In 1941, my husband decided to enlist as a radioman in the European Theater. It made some crooked kind of sense and restored peace on the home front.

"While stationed in England he used his multi-lingual skills, in English, French and German, to help crush the Nazis. In Canada, I was digging up dirt on world leaders, industrialists, scientists, and money barons who were making fortunes off the war. Eventually our combined efforts would lead to a cache of information that would fill Oz's coffers and give us clout beyond anyone's wildest aspirations.

"Because of the secretive nature of my husband's work, our letters to each other were newsy and tame. We'd risk a few obscure sexual innuendoes, but no suggestive language or questions about fidelity. I was certain he was on the hunt. I wasn't. I also wasn't looking forward to his return—his agitation and outbursts. Don't get me wrong, life wasn't easy. The war meant more work and less food, fuel, and comfort; but for the first time in my life, I was in charge and . . . well . . . I liked it.

"When the Germans surrendered on May 8th it was the beginning of the end of that wretched war. The week after, there was this wild eruption of energy and goodwill. Everyone seemed animated, excited, busy . . . in love! The radio carried hope—marching-band victory songs, a little ragtime and lots of jazz. On one of those nights, I tucked my daughter into bed, turned on the radio, and started cleaning the fireplace. I was covered with soot when I heard a tentative knock at the back door. Standing on the other side of the patched screen was my younger sister. She started to smile, then broke into tears. Not shy, my sister had always been generous and outgoing; but when it came to feelings, she was incredibly selfish and guarded. Our parents called her The Crypt. God save the person who told her it wouldn't hurt if she smiled or cried. The year before, after her fiancé was killed by enemy fire in France, she became the walking dead—no emotion, no tears. Nothing seemed to matter. Worried, I encouraged her to join the Oz group in Toronto. I thought it would loosen her grief, give her a reason to live.

"Stunned by her tears, I didn't unlatch the door until she asked if she could come in. When I pulled her in and gave her a hug, she completely lost it. She sobbed through pots of tea and shortbread cookies at the kitchen table. We talked for hours, early into the morning.

"My sister said she met her fire starter at Oz's New Year's Eve party. Over the six months since then, they'd seen each other once or twice a month. The war had a curious effect on time and sparked a *carte blanche* attitude about living large, taking advantage of what little joy came our way.

"I still remember her words. She said, 'We thought. No, scratch that. He said, *What the hell? We might all be dead by tomorrow. Why not make love, make memories?* I'm not stupid. I knew it was a line. My friends and I mocked girls who dropped their pants. But I was unbearably lonely. And suddenly I didn't care if it was a one-nighter. I didn't care if I was stupid.'

"Then the bomb. My sister told me her fire starter, Jacques, was handsome, funny, smart, single . . . and maybe rich. Jacques didn't know he was about to become a father."

Clearing her throat, Catherine said, "There was no way my sister was going to end up in a hell-hole unwed mother's home; or suffer the indignity of being a non-person because some uptight bureaucrats with fast zippers decided 'loose' women were undisciplined, unstable, and unfit to mother a child. We had to come up with a plan. I knew Jacques; I'd go with her to talk to him. We did. Jacques offered money and support, but no marriage—they barely knew each other. He offered to cover the cost of boarding school for my daughter if I was willing to help my sister navigate through the next six months."

Maggie's feet were bouncing up and down like Buddy Rich's sticks on a snare drum. Jacques was slumped forward in his chair, head down. Everyone else was looking from Catherine to Maggie to Jacques.

"My sister and I moved to Plan B. We'd lean on our older, reasonably wealthy, and very Catholic sister in Windsor. We'd take the train in August before the baby bump was too big to hide 'her sin.' By then, my daughter would be at boarding school. And, fortuitously, we had a war-effort-reason to be away. Our sister's husband was being shipped back to Windsor in July with a war injury. She'd need help in their three-story home.

"We decided to wait until we arrived in Windsor to explain the pregnancy. We couldn't risk the chance she'd call her priest and turn this into a religious crusade."

Catherine folded her hands and shook her head as if trying to discharge a memory before she said, "Jacques will pick it up from here."

Clyde watched Jacques scan the room as if he was assessing the emotional temperature. Was he waiting for permission to talk, or preparing to ask forgiveness for what he did, or for what he was about to say? Clyde was sure his teenage sons had heard about the *we-could-be-dead-by-tomorrow* line from the lips of Vietnam draftees who'd fixated on their libido, lottery number, and nightly news. Clyde couldn't remember if he used that line before he was drafted—before facing the horror of war, before going AWOL, before being rescued by Jacques.

*Ah, men—the species who hunt, crush, kill, destroy, and break hearts*, thought Clyde. For the first time since arriving in Toronto, his insidious man-guilt struck. The kind of slanted blame guys accept because they know they've somehow screwed up. Understanding this twisted psychology didn't help. Clyde was steeling himself to accept responsibility for Maggie's anger, Jacques' deceit, and Catherine's pain.

Finally, Jacques leaned forward and said, "Like Catherine, I thought I was ready to pick this up . . . tell you about it from my side; but . . . well . . . I've hidden it so long, I just now heard . . . realized . . . how complex and tender this story is. I'm ashamed to say, when

I met with Catherine and her sister, I felt trapped, like I was the victim. I was an asshole.

"Later, I blamed my crass behavior on my youth; but I knew young people who acted with moral courage and restraint. Then, I tried to write it off as recklessness; I was just a guy looking for a little action. It was far worse than that.

"I'm not asking for understanding or forgiveness. For decades I expected those I love most to carry this burden of untruth—this bizarre melodrama. I convinced myself we'd all be safer; Oz would be more powerful. That might have been the case in the beginning, but after a while, the falsehoods took over, twisted my thinking.

"So there's no doubt, I'm the Jacques in Catherine's story. The lounge lizard who seduced a young woman still reeling from the death of her fiancé on the battlefield. She was beautiful, kind, smart and funny. But this seduction wasn't about looking for a new romance or getting laid. This seduction was a sick, unholy, manipulation of a young woman who . . . who trusted me, who thought she could love again. For me, she was a ticket, a door, a way to get close to the woman I wanted, Anna.

"When Anna and Raymond Soulier joined Oz in the late-thirties, I was in bliss! Both were smart, funny, and rigorous in their discipline to do whatever needed getting done. Over the years, we played and worked together. Raymond and I loved sailing the Seaway. And Anna and I scavenged old supply warehouses, junkyards, and rummage sales to furnish Oz's safe houses and offices.

"Occasionally, Anna invited me to their place for dinner. The first few times, I brought a date; but soon discovered Raymond was one of those guys who considers new people an intrusion, women an affront. Rude and often belligerent, Raymond seemed to take callous pleasure ridiculing my consorts. Anna did her best to counteract his behavior, but it took far too much effort. I stopped bringing the latest woman in my life.

"Before long, Anna and I began to acknowledge our attraction to one other. Of course, we fought it. Anna, Raymond and I were good friends; she and Raymond were married with a young daughter. We knew it wouldn't work. But dreamers and lovers aren't always stopped by rational thoughts.

"After Raymond was stationed in England in 1941, his annual furlough brought him back to Canada for two weeks over the Christmas holidays. By December 1944, the war years had given Anna and me more than three years of relative freedom for our furtive romance. I'd never known anyone, man or woman, who captured my full attention until Anna came into my life. Never hungry or obsessive, our love was light and energetic.

"With Raymond's furlough coming up, I wanted Anna and me to confront him. Anna wanted to end our relationship. I didn't understand why she wanted to stay with a man who was angry, unpredictable, and often cruel. Anna told me her decision had nothing to do with what she wanted. Raymond was still her husband and Issie's father. She was convinced if she left him, she and Issie would spend the next ten years on the run. Anna thought her only option was to stir the embers of their marriage and manage Raymond's demons and outbursts until Issie was on her own. After that, Anna said, she'd be free to do what she wanted. What we both underestimated was Raymond's intelligence, patience, fury, and stealth."

# 20

# Boxing Day

THURSDAY AFTERNOON, SEPTEMBER 22, 1977—When Jacques looked up, Maggie was staring at him, perhaps through him. Everyone else was staring at Maggie. Jacques resisted an urge to jump up, wrap his arms around her, tell her everything would be okay. He didn't know if everything would be okay. Probably not. And there was more to tell. Jacques wanted Maggie to hear what he was about to say—raw and unencumbered by his neediness.

Taking a sip of water, Jacques sat taller. He imagined himself at the summit of a black-diamond ski run filled with Volkswagen-sized moguls covered in ice. He was about to take a flying leap of faith in his ability to carve the edges around, and over, and down.

"On the third day of Raymond's 1944 furlough, he came by my office and insisted I join his family for dinner on Boxing Day. For you Americans, it's the day after Christmas when employers in Old England gave their employees a gift in a box.

"Let me start over and reframe what I said. On the third day of Raymond's furlough, he *barged* into my office without stopping at the reception desk. When I asked him to have a seat, he shook his head no. He was . . . um . . . unclean and unshaven. His shirt was stained; his slacks tattered and dirty. Raymond pointed a shaking finger at me and yelled, 'Boxing Day. Dinner at my house. Six o'clock. No excuses!' Then he laughed softly, as if we'd just had a long, friendly conversation.

"I was a bit unnerved but wrote it off as jet lag. I said, 'Sure, Raymond! I look forward to getting an update . . .' Before I finished my sentence, Raymond seethed, 'That makes two of us,' then stormed out the door."

The room was silent except for Maggie's hiccups. Jacques caught Sam's eye, nodded, then turned to the group, "How about a short break to stretch our legs and visit the loo? I'll let Charles know he can drop off dessert . . . and, of course, a tip jar!"

After Maggie headed out the door, Clyde walked up to Sam and said, "How are you, my friend?"

"Angry. Angry that it's taking so long, that it's going too fast. Maggie's working so damn hard to keep it together. I'm afraid she'll have a stroke. At first, I thought it would be better to just come out with it—tell her if her parents are dead or alive. Now I can see it's more important for her to have the whole story. But it's so frigging heavy. Maggie hasn't had time to recover from her abduction, much less the plane crash and kidnapping. This could put her over the edge."

"What's that Finnish word you use to describe strength, resilience—sounds like sissy?"

"*Sisu?*"

"That's it." Maggie's got *sisu,* big time. You watch. She'll be the last person standing tonight."

When Maggie returned, all chatter stopped. She turned around to see if anyone was behind her, then threw her arms up, and said,

"Will you please . . . please stop coddling me. I've wanted this day for as long as I can remember. I expect it to be hard, probably gut-wrenching. If you want to spend this day with me, then buck up, and stop looking for signs of distress. I assure you I'm distressed. But I'm not going to turn into a puddle." Pointing at Sam, Maggie said, "And, Mr. Tervo, that includes you. I don't have the energy or interest to reassure anyone."

Loretta was the first one to start clapping. Within minutes, the sound of applause and smiles on her friends' faces brought Maggie to her knees. She started crying and laughing.

Helping her up, Sam whispered, "Brava, Maggie! You burst the damn and rebuilt the day. Do you have any idea how much I love you?"

Maggie studied his face, smiled, and said, "Of course."

Sam held onto her smile as if it was a talisman. His mood lifted and he found himself relaxing into the idea that everything would be fine.

Once they took their seats, Jacques said, "I want to thank Maggie for her bold, honest response to our individual and collective caretaking. I know, then forget, how uncomfortable it is when others think they know us better than we know ourselves. Which is quite a stretch, because we spend our lives trying to figure out who we are, and we seldom do."

Blanche said, "Amen, brother."

Jacques smiled and said, "Amen, Sister Blanche. I also want to report the girls made quite a haul—more than twenty bucks in tips. If you didn't get enough lemon meringue, you've got time. Charles is going to leave everything here until we break for dinner. And the girls and Emma are going to set up a girls-only camp in the cafeteria tonight. Catherine, any announcements I'm forgetting?"

"Tonight's menu. Charles and the girls are preparing shrimp with long-grained rice, coleslaw, and a pineapple right-side-up cake."

Jacques noted the fatigue in the room; the idea of another meal seemed like too much. "Let's see," he began, "where was I? Ah, yes. Raymond was storming out the door. I wanted to call Anna but knew that was risky. Issie was a precocious six-year-old and loved answering the phone. Over the previous year, Issie had given Anna and me report-outs of every person who called or stopped by the house. Then it hit me. All those months when Issie was perfecting her observation and reporting abilities, Anna and I had been letting down our guard. Of course, Raymond—the radioman—would be quizzing Issie, and Issie would be thrilled to have Raymond's attention. I was certain Raymond had already heard about the dinners we shared; where we went on our Sunday drives; how often I called; the gifts I brought. I was frantic. Anna and I needed to talk.

"Before I took off to find Anna, she showed up at my office door. We looked at each other with the sheer terror and humiliation of two people caught in the act.

"'Oh, god,' said Anna. 'Raymond went ballistic. If he shows up . . .'

"I said, 'Too late. He showed up and demanded I come to your house on Boxing Day for dinner. He was wired.'

"Anna said, 'That's good. You'll come on Boxing Day. We can change the story.'

"The silence between us was filled with unanswered threats. My mind was reeling. I wanted to be the man, take care of Anna and Issie. But Anna wanted something else. I whispered, 'What do you mean? How do we change the story?'

"Tears were streaming down Anna's face. She said, 'I'm going to seduce him with food, love and sex. I'll devote myself to his every need. When you come to dinner, I'll be as cold and disinterested in you as I can be. And you . . . you'll focus all your attention on Raymond. You'll ignore me and Issie to the extent that it breaks your heart. If you love me, if you want to protect me and Issie, you'll do this.'

"I wasn't sure I loved her enough to do what she asked of me, much less live with the fact she planned to give another man—husband or not—slavish devotion and sex. Anna must have mistaken me for a grown-up. God knows I wanted to be a renaissance man; but beneath the bard and bravado, I was a pimply-faced teenage boy when it came to women."

Loretta lifted her hands in supplication and hummed approval.

Nodding his head, Jacques said, "Loretta gets it. We men act like we've got it together, but inside we know we're just one high-heel-click away from rejection. That's where I was when Anna handed me a script to castrate myself. That was my first reaction. My second was I'd do anything to keep her in my life. I wiped Anna's tears with my handkerchief and told her I loved her; I'd do anything for her. I promised to become Raymond's best friend and stay away from her. I was sure my heart would never mend.

"Boxing Day dinner at the Souliers was like attending a Eugene O'Neill play. I felt plugged into every word, expression, motion as an observer; then got disoriented when Raymond invited me into the drama with a question. I say Raymond because he led the discussion. Let me correct that. Raymond was more like a puppeteer, pulling strings and controlling the conversation.

"He said, 'Anna, tell Jacques what you got in your box today.' Keeping her eyes on Raymond, Anna smiled and said, 'My husband gave me the most beautiful gossamer nightgown I've ever seen.' Then, touching Raymond's cheek, she whispered, 'To be sure, this gown was not intended for angels.'

"Raymond touched Anna's cheek, laughed and said, 'I've come a long way since the Boxing Days when my brothers and I boxed dead animals and left them on the front steps of houses. We'd ring the bell then hide behind bushes, hoping they'd open their *gift* outside. We were miserable little scamps, but got to admit, it was funny as hell.'

"Anna shook her head, laughed and said, 'Raymond Soulier, you and your brothers were miserable little scamps!' then sent a warning glance to me.

"'Your turn, Isabel,' said Raymond, 'tell Mr. Ruivivar what you found in your box.' Issie looked as if she was pouting; through gritted teeth, she said, 'My name is ISSIE, not Isabel!' In a flash, Raymond was out of his chair and lifting Issie up by her hair. Issie screamed. I was almost out of my chair when Anna shook her head sharply and I sat down.

"Anna said, 'My dear Isabel, we love calling you by your formal name. There's no need to be rude. Now, let's sit down. After you catch your breath, we'll hear about your gift.'

"I leaned across the table, I wanted to knock Raymond on his ass. Instead, I asked him if I could make a toast; he gave me a smirk. Taking my cues from Anna's focus on Raymond and her remarkable peace-keeping language, I said, 'To Raymond and all the other brave soldiers who risk their lives for us, to keep us safe. I'm very proud to know you and call you friend.'

"I could tell by Raymond's face he wasn't buying it, but he wasn't rejecting it. He looked curious, interested. As much as I wanted to rescue Anna and Issie from his abuse, I knew I was tipping at windmills. Anna made clear her intent to ride this out. I could accept it or lose her. I wasn't about to lose her.

"During the next few weeks, Anna began to change the story and work her miracles. She convinced Raymond to extend his furlough from two weeks to two months so they could spend time together and he could get a break from the constant stress of spying. I wasn't surprised when Raymond told me his command officer approved the two-month leave. Anyone who shared a cramped radio room or a city park with Raymond knew he was a headcase.

"Over time, Raymond and I became 'good friends' and Anna and I drifted further apart. Issie had a hard time accepting I was no longer a helpmate or playmate. Jigsaw puzzles were off-limits to me, and Raymond didn't have the disposition or patience for quiet play. I watched Anna take on more responsibility for stage-managing the right level of engagement and mix between her, Raymond, Issie, and me. She looked exhausted. I was close to empty—dating and bedding women whose names I'd forget; plunging myself in worry about Anna and Issie; or immersing myself in Oz. Each day I hoped Anna and I would cross paths, see each other in a meeting without Raymond, ride in the same elevator."

For several minutes, no one talked. Then Catherine said, "I think Jacques is ready for me to pick up the story and crank it up a bit. Besides my own anxiety about this part of the story, we have two people in our anteroom waiting for the sky to drop.

"When Anna showed up at Union Station in Toronto just before Christmas in 1959, it was after she'd spent almost ten years in captivity. Anna's captor was Raymond. Held hostage by the threat of brutality, he broke Anna's leg when she attempted to run away, sliced her face with a fishing knife after a stranger whistled at her, and smashed his fist into her teeth the one time she laughed at him. He broke her body, but not her soul. I know this because I am Anna."

Maggie thought this entire stage play was surreal. Her body felt like lead; as if separated from her emotions, her voice, her heart. Everyone in the room was looking at her, expecting what? *What does a normal person do when someone shows up and says, 'I'm your long-lost imagined mother; the one who's been hiding behind another name, another face, another character. Here I am, day-tripping on this planet in clear sight.'* Sam tried to touch her; she recoiled.

Maggie looked up. Catherine was sitting on a chair in front of her, knees to knees, holding her hands saying, "Maggie, please, hear me. I was born Anna and from the first moment I saw you, I loved you. When you were born, your mother couldn't keep you, so she and I let Raymond believe he was your father. It was the only way to keep peace. During your first five years, Raymond had moments of warmth and kindness, but never enough. You deserved more, Issie deserved more. For far too many years I felt like I had no choice. I was convinced Raymond would never let us live without him. I thought if I stayed with Raymond until you and Issie were out of high school—off and away to a college in the States—far away from Raymond—you'd be okay. But Raymond couldn't keep it together; his episodes got worse.

"Our sailing trip to Quebec, in the summer of 1950, was to get Raymond into a mental hospital. When he was settled, I planned to fly home to take you and Issie away, far away. But Raymond knew something wasn't right. Despite his demons and craziness, Raymond was smart, shrewd and suspicious. I'm sure he knew I felt trapped; that I could barely put up with him. It fed his cynicism and wrath. When I suggested a long, romantic sailing trip for our fifteenth wedding anniversary, Raymond prepared for Armageddon. Gun-toting pirates in a fiberglass speedboat picked us up on the Seaway. Jacques had agreed to take charge if I went missing. He and your Aunt Minnie had the resources and shared responsibility to take care of you and Issie."

Maggie was still gasping for breath when Anna/Catherine finished talking, but she felt calmer. This brave, determined, woman risked her life to save hers and Issie's futures. Her imagined mother was loving, generous, brave and kind. *Then why,* thought Maggie, *do I want to pick up both my feet and shove Anna and her wheeled chair across the goddamn room?*

"Earlier, when you talked about your younger sister showing up at your door. Was that Aunt Jo?" asked Maggie.

"Yes, it was Jo."

"Does that mean Aunt Jo is my mother?"

"Yes, Jo is your mother."

"And my father . . .?"

When Anna touched her face, Maggie felt the heat of Anna's fingertips and watched her life pass through Anna's eyes. Maggie was sure everyone heard blood racing to her heart.

"Yes, my love . . . Jacques is your father."

Maggie's entire body started to shake; her feet pedaled the floor. She didn't want to collapse, not now. She forced herself to focus.

"And, Raymond, where is he? Is he still alive?"

"We don't know."

"Does Issie know who you are?"

Anna nodded, then whispered, "She does now."

After carefully unfolding her hand from Maggie's, Anna backed her chair up and left the room. When Sam offered his hand to Maggie to stand up, she kicked both his knees with the full force of unleashed anger.

"Jesus, Maggie. I had no idea Catherine was Anna. I wasn't keeping anything from you."

"I know. But you're the only person I can kick right now. The only one."

Sam saw the pain, confusion, and determination in Maggie's eyes. He offered both his hands, helped her up and said, "I know, babe . . . I'm one lucky guy." Then he smiled his smile. And Maggie smiled back.

Before Anna/Catherine returned, Jacques asked everyone to take their seats and said, "For reasons you might now imagine, but beyond our scope to question, Catherine will not change her name. She asks that you continue to call her Catherine and I'm sure you'll honor her request.

"Before we break, I want you to consider that Jo and Issie will be occupying seats they never intended to fill. Like most of us, they made decisions and promises they thought they had to make when they were young and threatened by circumstances, or people who controlled their lives.

"Maggie, I know you've been whipsawed by these revelations, and we've watched you handle them with intelligence and grace. I hope you'll hang onto those attributes tonight. Our discussions are difficult, maybe mind-blowing; but, to a person, everyone is showing up because of their love and respect for you. Because we want to keep you in our lives. Marguerite, you have every right to be angry and speak your truth. But, beyond that, I hope you'll . . . hmm . . . not walk away from me, from our highly-dysfunctional, well-intentioned family."

# 21

# No Empty Chairs

THURSDAY EVENING, SEPTEMBER 22, 1977—No lap meals. Dinner was two hours away and Charles was taking advantage of their break to set up a dinner table with earthenware and linen napkins. Maggie's stomach was turning with anxiety and hunger. For sure she was hyped about seeing Issie; she could hardly wait to wrap her arms around her. With or without a common parent, they were raised as sisters. But why, Maggie wondered, was she furious with Anna because she's not her mother? What in god's name will she do when she sees Aunt Jo? Kick her in the knees?

Maggie joined Loretta and Blanche at the windowed wall and watched streetlights sketch shadows across the harbor. "When I played my mind games, once or twice I wondered if Aunt Jo was my mother. But it didn't feel right. So much for psychic pulls. What I can't understand is how she and Anna conned Raymond into thinking Anna was my mother. I was born months after the war ended, after Raymond was discharged."

Just then, Sam called her name and waved her over. Standing in the open door, he said "Hey, Mag, you okay?" Maggie banged her forehead on his shoulder without a word; Sam knew that was code for 'don't even think about going there.'

"Okay, babe, I got it. Catherine and I just talked. You might want to consider a change in plans for tonight. She'll bring you up to speed in the hallway. If I don't see you in five minutes, I'll know you've decided on Plan B and let everyone know they've got time to check on their kids, call home. I'll use the time to check on Tekla and call Ma."

Maggie gave Sam a few dismissive pats on the shoulder and walked through the door.

To Maggie, Catherine looked weary from so much truth-telling and time travel. To Catherine, Maggie looked like she was on autopilot.

"I hope you'll find a way to forgive me, to forgive us," said Catherine. "We wanted to meet your timeline for these talks, but we might have been too optimistic. Issie and Jo want to meet with you, me, and Jacques first. The originating characters in our historical novel if you will. Make sense?"

Maggie nodded her head. Not because it made sense, but because she flashed on the idea that life wasn't supposed to make sense. What happens between the prologue and epilogue is only one person's story—one person's disorderly, ratcheted notion of reality. What matters is truth; that liminal, often taunted veracity that shines between the paragraphs, lines and words of every person's story.

When Catherine and Maggie walked into the anteroom, Jacques was leaning across the coffee table talking to Aunt Jo and Issie. They all stopped leaning and talking. Maggie thought Aunt Jo looked twenty years older in her *de rigueur* black sheath dress and colorful shawl. Her stunning mid-length, white hair looked untended; her face smeared by mascara and tears. Issie, dressed in black corduroy bells and an aqua sweater, appeared fresh-faced, expectant, vibrant—maybe a little intoxicated.

Before Maggie had time to conjugate her mother-daughter relationship with Aunt Jo, Issie jumped up and hugged her tight, whispering, "Maggie, oh Maggie. I'm so sorry. I knew and I couldn't tell you. I tried. Honestly, I tried. When I said Jacques was kinder to you. When I hinted Jacques and Anna might have had an affair. I promised not to tell, but I knew it was tearing you up and I wanted to tell you what I knew. But I couldn't. Until this week, I promise, I thought Anna was somewhere with Raymond. I had no idea Aunt Jo was your mother." When Issie began to cry, Maggie felt Issie's pain and remorse as if it were her own. Issie had been grieving for her parents. Maggie was still grieving for Issie's parents because they were the only parents she'd known. This time, Maggie's tears were for Issie, for all of them.

Jacques leaned forward and said, "One question, Issie. What did you see or hear that you promised not to tell, that haunted you for these many years?"

"When I was eight, Maggie was just starting to walk. We were in small park. I wanted to play on the teeter-totter and Anna was worried about watching me and Maggie at the same time. Just then, Anna saw you sitting on a park bench and asked if you'd watch Maggie for a bit."

Nodding, Jacques smiled and said, "I remember that lovely summer day."

"When we got to the teeter-totters, Anna saw my bare feet and sent me back to get my shoes. My sandals were behind the bench you and Maggie were sitting on. I knew if Maggie saw me, she'd go bonkers, so I tried creeping up behind the bench to reach my shoes. I heard you say something like, 'My little beauty, you might never know I'm your papa. And you won't remember this, but I want to tell you I love you.' I felt jealous because you called Maggie 'little beauty,' because being her papa meant you loved her more than me. I was deep in my center-of-the-universe evolutionary phase, so I hung on to each of your words to torment myself year . . . after year . . . after year."

Jacques shook his head, "I can imagine. Eight is such a vulnerable age. I hope one day you'll understand how much we both loved you and fought against our self-imposed exile. Like Maggie, you were a victim of decisions far beyond your reach or comprehension. Tell me, Issie, who did you promise not to tell?"

Issie looked at Anna, now Catherine, who nodded her head, and Issie replied, "A few weeks after the park day, I was pitching a fit because I couldn't find my sandals and Anna got down on the floor with me and said, 'Issie Belle, what on earth are you so angry about?' Issie Belle was her pet name for me since I was a baby. She hadn't called me Issie Belle in a long time; it stopped me cold. I started sobbing like a baby. She held me in her arms, rocked me, and whispered, 'It's okay, it's okay. You can tell me.' I blurted out what I heard you say on the park bench.

"Anna started to cry and said something like, 'Oh, my very grown-up Issie Belle, I'm sorry you waited to tell me. That's a big secret to keep. I always thought you were good at keeping secrets, but now I know how good you are.' And the rest I remember word-for-word. Anna said, 'We womenfolk keep secrets to keep peace in our house. With Raymond's demons, it's the only way. You know that as well as I do. I'm so glad you told me. Now, I'm going to ask you to keep that secret for the rest of your life, Issie Belle. It's a big promise, but I know you can keep it.'

"Anna trusted me, and I held that trust like a pearl, a gift from my mother. When Maggie begged me to go back in time, to tell her what I remembered, I thought about Anna sitting on the floor and treating me like an equal."

Struck by the raw tenderness, courage and faith of families held by secrets and promises, Maggie looked around the room. The mix of smiles and tears on each of their faces seemed both absurd and reasonable—as if permitting sorrow was the key to joy.

Jo patted the sofa and Maggie slid in next to her. Up close Maggie saw Jo's bloodshot eyes and sallow skin. For someone who'd been so strong and vital, she looked old and frail. Catherine sat on Jo's other side holding her hand.

Once everyone was seated around the narrow coffee table, Jo said, "Let me start with truth and make every effort to never again move away from truth . . . or deny truth . . . or blame others for my untruths.

"On October 26, 1945, when I kissed Marguerite and placed her in Anna's arms, I thought I would die of grief and shame. Until this week, I was certain Anna was dead. When I thought I'd lost contact with Maggie, Sam and Tekla, I was convinced it was because of my panicked warnings about Jacques and Catherine. You see, my life's work, my sole purpose in being, was to keep these secrets buried. If I didn't, I'd lose everyone I loved. No doubt this reunion and these revelations will tax my life with regret for having kept these secrets. No; forget I said that. Screw regret! Starting today, I stop hiding and apologizing for my past and begin to live my life in technicolor.

"Let me start by liberating you from any misconception I wasn't responsible for the choices I made during the war. I was a determined, self-centered young woman. Not worldly, but I'd read *The Scarlet Letter* and understood the economics of war. Men were being killed off by the thousands. I'd already lost the love of my life and understood the concept of scarce resources. We were losing men every day."

Jo took Maggie's hand and spoke directly to her: "I've been crying for the past two days wondering how I was going to reintroduce myself to you, my extraordinary daughter. Here, in front of your mother—my very brave, very determined big sister Anna—and the only mother you've known. The woman who took you in, loved you and raised you as her own. No one can take that away from you or Anna. No other woman has bonded with you, loved you, taken care of you more than Anna. Whatever I might say, or do, or think, Anna is your mother. My hope is you and I will find other ways to mend and weave.

"When Phillip died in June 1944, I thought my life was over. There's no way to describe my desolation when I heard he was killed by enemy fire. But that's untrue. Phillip wasn't killed by enemy fire. I chose those words because they were the cleanest, kindest way to tell people, to tell myself. The callous truth is, following the Normandy invasion, more than one hundred and fifty Canadian POWs were executed by the 12th SS Panzer Division, Hitler's Youth; little boys groomed to be killers.

"Near the charming old village of Authie, France, it's easy to imagine Phillip thinking life as a POW might be a tough go; but he believed the war was coming to an end. No doubt he expected the Germans to be on fire with rage after the Normandy landing, but the Geneva Convention protected prisoners of war. On June 7th, the Wehrmacht randomly selected eleven Canadian POWs and marched them to the *Abbaye d'Ardenne* garden—near the gothic church that served as headquarters for the SS commander. Overgrown, neglected shrubs would have been brimming with life, as daylilies pushed another year's bloom through stinging nettle. You see, Phillip wasn't killed by enemy fire. Phillip was marched to a holy place and assassinated by well-groomed boys. Dust to dust, ashes to ashes."

When Maggie looked up, Jo was the only one with dry eyes. Nodding at Jacques, Jo turned back to Maggie and continued, "Six months later I convinced myself I wanted to live. The Nazi's killed Phillip, but they weren't going to kill me. Anna introduced me to Oz, and I met Jacques Ruivivar. Jacques thought he was courting me, but in truth, I was trying to seduce him. I was so hungry for connection, love, intimacy, it was impossible to play it cool. I know Anna takes responsibility for introducing me—and Jacques takes responsibility for seducing me—but I want each of you to know I was not an *ingénue*. I was a young woman with a career in merchandising, and . . . I was not a pushover or a virgin. I had sex with Jacques because I wanted to. I got pregnant and hoped he would marry me. That's not what he wanted. To make it sadder and more complex, I didn't know Jacques was in love with my married sister Anna.

"Believe me when I say I've cried far too many tears over my lies, my shame, my pretending to be a chaste woman-of-good-standing. Beyond all the self-recriminations, my hope is that you, my beautiful Marguerite, will understand why I gave you to my sister.

"As an unwed pregnant woman in 1945, I risked losing you in a forced adoption. In Canada, we knew or heard about unwed mothers whose babies were ripped out of their arms to be given or, we suspected, sold to a family with a mother and father. No doubt, Raymond was certifiable, but my sister Anna . . . she was an angel, and I knew . . . somehow . . . I knew Jacques would be in the wings. My prayer was that one day I'd get to know you, help you if I could. We'd all be family. I couldn't be your mother, but I could be Aunt Jo. It was something. I know how . . . stretched this must seem; but the years we lived together in Detroit were the most vital years of my life.

"If you want to assign blame for our broken family, blame me. I forced the decision. It won't change how much I love you, or how much Issie and Anna, now Catherine, love you. And my dear Marguerite, fate was on our side when it led me to Jacques. I know he's fallen deeply in love with you, Sam, and Tekla. For too long, I tried to keep you and Jacques apart because I was afraid. I'm no longer afraid and I hope you'll forgive me."

Maggie slipped back in time. During her undergraduate and graduate years at Wayne State, she slept in Aunt Jo's attic and shared her lively, colorful home. Aunt Jo's kitchen table was the epicenter—from making fun of their pettiness and pufferies to struggling with the inconsolable wretchedness of assassinations that marked time in the sixties. Yet, it was as if Maggie was seeing Aunt Jo's eyes for the first time. Dark green, flecked in gold, like hers; the pain living in Aunt Jo's eyes, like her own.

Maggie wanted her words to reflect Jacques' confidence in her intelligence and grace. *Where to begin?* she wondered, then started by translating her thoughts into words.

"I want to reflect Jacques' confidence in my intelligence and grace. Of course, you've each seen me act dumb on both sides—but I'm determined to become an adult. For too many years, I thought ALL OF THIS was about me. Of course, it's not. Now, I want to meet you where you are, not where I've planted you in my mind's diorama."

Maggie reached her hand across the table and took Issie's hand. "My beautiful, badass sister. You did try to warn me about the untruths. But, even if you'd known and kept quiet, how could I not love you? That in no way means we'll always agree or get along, but it does mean I'm not going to dump you for another sister. *Capisce?*"

Issie studied Maggie's face before she nodded, shrugged her shoulders, and said, "Okay, but no horse heads in my bed. Too creepy."

Catherine laughed so hard she snorted. "Oh my god, Issie, you've grown up to be me. I can't wait to meet the boys and look for dust balls under your sofa."

"Yes!" laughed Maggie, "Issie is like you. And Jo's right; absent or not, you've been a mother to me for over thirty years. When we met again, in 1968, I didn't trust myself to cross the line and ask if you were Anna. I think I was so intent, so committed to my livelong saga, so . . . hmm . . . perversely entertained, I didn't want to disrupt it with the truth. Thank you for helping me over that hump.

"And Mr. Ruivivar. In my twenties, I sometimes played with the idea you were my father. Distinguished, successful, smart, good-looking, how could I go wrong? But I'd write it off as a ruse. I don't recall much about Raymond. He seemed to be gone a lot. But one memory, repetitive dream, involves someone who looks like you carrying me as a toddler down a narrow cobblestone street. A woman is calling out 'take her, she's yours!' No, she was speaking French, she said, '*Prenez-la, elle est à vous!*'"

All eyes were on Jacques as he stared at Maggie with such compassion no one wanted to break the spell. Jacques whispered, "You remember that evening?"

"I don't know. When I dream about it, it's an evening, cool, maybe misty. It feels real. I'm in a red wool coat with a matching bonnet."

"When you were just starting to walk, Raymond was having an episode. That's what we called them, episodes. But they were violent, frightening eruptions. Anna ran out of the house with you and Issie. After she dropped Issie with a neighbor, Anna found me at a local pub and waved me out. She was frantic. She placed you in my arms and said, 'Hurry. Take her, she's yours.' Anna was on her way to a safe house that Oz kept in Toronto. She couldn't bring children. Maggie, you and I spent three days together, until Raymond was safely confined in a mental ward. Once on medication, Raymond would do well and get released. After a few weeks, he'd rail against his meds because he thought Anna was trying to poison him."

"If only I had," said Catherine. "I know that sounds vicious, but there was no help for people with demons or their families. The police were powerless. Unless Raymond hurt me, or someone else, there was nothing they could do. It was up to me. At the first sign from Raymond—tightening or pounding his fist, going batshit over some small slight—I'd wait for my first chance to grab Issie and Maggie and run like there was no tomorrow.

"That particular night there was a fog. It was misty and other-worldly. I thought how nice for you and Jacques to bond; how lovely for each of us to have a few days of peace."

Warmed by the inclusion of kindreds, Maggie watched and listened to her peculiar family bring up other episodes and flights—ice cream parties and civil rights marches. When Maggie covered Jo's hand with her own, she felt a definitive Darwinian wink, a quiet contentment. They looked at each other and Maggie knew words would either be redundant or not enough. She wondered, *has the cradle finally stopped rocking the tree?*

Catherine waved to get Maggie's attention and said, "What say you, Ms. Maggie? Do we continue rehearsing or bring this act to the big stage?"

Maggie looked at Jo. Letting go of Maggie's hand, Jo stood up, rewrapped her shawl with a matador's flair, and proclaimed, "Big stage? You're kidding me, right? I say Broadway! No one can touch us when it comes to high drama. Besides, I'm half-starving. What's for dinner?"

# 22

# Catalytic Converters

THURSDAY NIGHT, SEPTEMBER 22, 1977—When Maggie and her reconstituted kin filed into the meeting room, the lights were turned down. Loretta, Blanche, Clyde and Sam were standing at the bar inhaling salted nuts and reading headlines under an Anglepoise lamp. On the opposite side of the room, the dinner table held a dozen white votive candles dancing across the starlit harbor-view.

Catherine stepped forward and said, "This has been a long week and an exceptionally long day. Jacques and I thought a relaxed dinner and evening makes more sense. What if we cover a few unanswered questions and some of today's headlines after we eat, and leave the wrap-up and plan-of-action decisions for tomorrow?"

The response sounded like a choreographed group-sigh. Although relieved, and satisfied in a way she never imagined, Maggie knew she was running on empty. Sam walked up, put his arm around her waist, nuzzled her neck and whispered, "You okay?"

"Yes, I'm good. We all spoke from our hearts and seemed to understand each other's point of view. It was mind-blowing—far more loving than I thought possible."

"In what way?"

"It was almost like stripping off all the ids we've worn and seeing each other uncensored."

"Like a catalytic converter scrubbing the air?"

Maggie's look didn't need word props; Sam knew she was loaded for bear. "Drop it, Tervo. I know there are no easy answers. I'm using shorthand because . . . because . . . screw you." Maggie turned and marched out of the room.

Clyde walked up to Sam and looked him in the eye. Sam shrugged his shoulders and said, "I used my catalytic converter schtick because I didn't want her to get too comfortable about their love fest. Probably not the right time or place. Okay . . . I'm a dickhead."

"Yes, you are, my friend. Go find her and give her the hug she was looking for. If we don't eat soon, I'll have a meltdown. And if you use the catalytic converter schtick to help me out, I'll kick your sorry ass. Any questions?"

By the time everyone settled at the dinner table, Charles, Emma and the three girls entered the room and began serving dinner.

Tekla placed Maggie's plate in front of her and said, "We hope you enjoy your meal, madame. Please let me know if you need any con-de-mints."

"Why thank you Tekla. What kind of con-de-mints do you have?"

"You can choose red sauce or white sauce."

"Sounds wonderful! May I have one of each?"

Tekla huffed as she walked away from the table to ask Emma if Maggie could have both kinds of sauce. When Tekla returned to the table and placed two cruets next to Maggie's plate, she said,

"Excuse me for taking so long, madame, but you're the one who asked for both sauces. Is that quite enough?"

Maggie bit back her laughter and said, "Merci buckets! You're very good at your job."

Tekla giggled and said, "Merci buckets to you!"

Once the girls were gone, and dinner dishes cleared, Catherine asked Charles to wait until the morning to set up the room.

Helping herself to dessert, Maggie smiled. The to-die-for pineapple-right-side-up cake, jammed into cupcakes, seemed the perfect metaphor for this day.

Jacques raised his glass and said, "Before we begin, I'd like to propose a toast to our remarkable progress. We pushed through decades of societal mandates, missteps, crimes, emotional warfare and brutality. We were informed or reminded that genetics, alone, doesn't make families. Who we are, how we relate, how we form families and communities is based on our energy and facility to connect with one another. Each of you has proven this and I'm honored to be a part of this forced, but otherwise timely, reunion. *Santé!*"

"*Santé!*" The group toasted in return.

"Is anyone willing to give us an overview of the headlines?" asked Catherine.

Loretta raised her hand and said, "A quick review. The papers were slow to make it to the third floor. Apparently, the courier left them on the loading dock and security was waiting for him to ring the bell."

"A quick review works for me," said Catherine. "I don't think anyone has the energy to make a deep dive."

"Okay, off the top of my head. Toronto, Windsor and Hamilton headlines focused on 'Victims of Plane Crash Found Alive' with reports that Sam and Tekla were in good health and cooperating with the aviation authorities and Toronto Police in their investigations. Nothing about Oz or the juicers. From our Detroit neighbors,

'Canadian Radicals Target *La Bière.*' The reporter covered the illegal preservative claim in a few lines. After that, he goes into a tirade about Oz." Picking up the Detroit paper, Loretta read, "'Oz, a wannabe-militant underground threat, spent decades mocking the British Monarchy. Now, they're aiming their slingshots at an American pastime.'"

"I wonder how many cases of beer that cost? What are the economics when it comes to wholesale death by poisoning?" said Clyde.

"Oz fared better in New York," said Loretta. "The headline reads, 'Kidnapped Americans Rescued by Human Rights Group,' with a generous, mostly accurate history of Oz's work. But there's nothing about the juicers. Other than Detroit's reference to a preservative, no one mentioned preservatives or DEPC. I got the drift no one took time to read the documents, much less, run them through their own traps. Maybe we underestimated the power of the breweries and/or the newspapers; both must have had something to gain or lose in their bargain with the devil."

"Let's hope not. We'll keep a close eye on the media for the next few months. My take is their legal counsels advised caution until they've got something to back up Oz's report," said Catherine.

"We're talking big money and uncharted territory," said Clyde. "We ran into serious pushback by the press when we broke the story about black gold fueling the Vietnam War."

Jo waved her hand and said, "Any chance we can move to the unanswered questions? I'm flat-out exhausted and have nothing to add to this part of the discussion."

"Same here," said Issie.

"Me too," said Maggie. "I have one follow-up question. After that, I want a pillow."

"You've got the floor," said Catherine.

"No doubt I've got a lot to take in, to comprehend, and thank each of you for being here, for caring about me. Stuck in adolescence most of my life, I finally, mercifully grokked that this whole thing was not just about me. Amazing, isn't it—how twisted I was in my own, worried little history? Today, I learned it's more a tale about how we each survived the dark ages of our lives—the ignorance, fear, religious and social mores that marginalize and contain us.

"To Loretta, Clyde, Blanche—my best friends and Detroit Eight family—I promise to fill you in on my private meeting with relatives. But for tonight, if you haven't already heard, I'm here with my mother, Catherine; my birth mother, Aunt Jo; my sister/cousin, Issie; and my birth father, Jacques." Maggie noticed there was no intake of breath.

"No surprise?" asked Maggie.

Clyde leaned forward and said, "Sorry, Maggie. I meant to tell you when you came in that I used my press-release knowledge to give Blanche and Loretta a short ancestry course."

Maggie nodded her head and said, "Ah! That makes it easier. So . . . my question to Catherine and Jo is . . . how did you convince Raymond I was his daughter?"

Catherine looked at Jo, who pointed at Catherine. "We got lucky," Catherine began. "When Jo showed up at my door in May 1945, the week after the German's surrendered, she calculated she became pregnant with you late in January, which—as you know—meant a late October delivery. During Raymond's extended leave, we had sex at least twice in late January. Because my periods were irregular, there was no way to map out abstinence or predict ovulation and Raymond refused to use condoms. At first, Raymond and I laughingly referred to intercourse as 'tossing the dice.' Later, when Raymond was fighting his demons—mean, drunk, and crazy—he'd call me names and say, 'get ready to toss the dice.' My solar plexus would freeze; my fight or flight response iced. After we conceived Issie Belle, I never got pregnant. I thought it was because Raymond and I couldn't produce enough love to conceive. Now I realize it was more likely a combination of my tipped uterus and the effect of his anti-psychotic drugs. Issie Belle was my light, my courage. I worried about bringing a new baby into our chaotic home, but family is family. I still held the childish fantasy I could change other people and MAKE them happy. I thought I could love Raymond enough to fix him; love you and Issie enough to keep you safe. I was so determined—so convinced by my single-minded power to change the world—that I ended up losing my way and my daughters."

Issie took Maggie's hand and held it. *Still my big sister,* thought Maggie, as she leaned her head on Issie's shoulder.

Drawn by the tenderness of their silent exchange, Catherine smiled and said, "But, my daughters always knew they were sisters! Where was I? Ah . . . yes. Jo and I had timing and luck on our side. The next hurdle was hiding Jo's pregnancy and creating my own. Jo was long-waisted and physically fit. We thought she could eat less and hide her pregnancy until August, which was pushing it a bit. In the meantime, I'd eat more, wear bulky clothes and tell Raymond and our neighbors about my pregnancy. Because of Raymond's extended leave over the Christmas holidays, he wouldn't head back to Toronto until mid-September. Once Jacques offered to pay for Issie's boarding school, it all seemed possible.

"Late that June, I wrote Raymond and told him Issie was one of three girls selected to attend Amadeus boarding school on a scholarship beginning in August. And Jo and I thought it best if we stayed with my sister Minnie for a few months because her husband Cyp would need help with his war injury, and I'd need help after I delivered. Raymond knew their three-story home was a nightmare to navigate and keep clean. At six feet, Minnie was taller than most men in our generation and suffered from arthritic knees that made her meaner than dirt. When you combined her meanness with her Catholic piety, there was no uncertainty in Minnie's good-bad holy wars. She suffered no losses. Cyp was seven inches shorter than Minnie with a remarkable sense of humor and patience. No one quite understood why Cyp and Minnie adored one another.

"For Raymond there was no love lost when it came to Minnie. The last time he saw her was the first Sunday in November 1937. I remember because I was pregnant with Issie and suffering my first bout of morning sickness. When Minnie called us for breakfast, she saw Raymond shaking his fist at me in anger. Picking up her iron skillet, still hot from buttermilk pancakes, Minnie whipped the skillet over her head and chased Raymond out the door. The icy landing hurled him down six concrete steps and produced a painful baker's cyst behind his right knee. At the same time each succeeding year, Raymond's knee popped with a baker's cyst. He was convinced Minnie was a witch. Raymond didn't notice that every year, on the first Sunday of November, I'd pull out my biggest iron skillet and make buttermilk pancakes.

"With that, you'll better understand why Minnie's house became my safe house before Oz opened one in Toronto. If this had simply been the humiliation of a woman scaring him off, Raymond would have eventually confronted and intimidated Minnie in her own home. But, as predictably, unpredictable as Raymond might have been—he was predictably scared straight by witchcraft. Minnie, Jo and I knew we could work this to our advantage."

# 23

# Rain Cheques

FRIDAY MORNING, SEPTEMBER 23, 1977—*French poets attempt to salvage the post-lovemaking-trace-of-rapture that survives sleep for one exasperating-ephemeral-nanosecond upon wakening. There's no way to replicate this liminal ecstasy, but it doesn't stop lovers from trying or poets from writing aubades,* thought Maggie.

Eyes still closed against the morning sun and that transient nanosecond, Sam began blindly and wildly patting the bed in search of her. Maggie laughed, threw her right leg over his back and began kissing his neck and nibbling his ear until someone knocked at the door.

"Maggie?" called a female voice.

Maggie threw on her robe, cracked open the door. Emma, dressed in jeans and a sweatshirt said, "I'm sorry to disturb you and Sam so early, but the girls and Charles decided to make brioche French toast, sausage, and blueberry compote. To say they got carried away is, well, ridiculously understated. We're asking everyone to join us in the cafeteria in fifteen to twenty minutes. The Maple Leaf Pensione group—including the Webster boys—are heading this way."

"Sounds delicious! We'll see you soon."

After the door clicked shut, Maggie turned, untied her robe and let it fall off her shoulders. Her eyes were on Sam watching her. Maggie approached him with slow, exaggerated, colt-like leg lifts and stretches before she mounted him. Before he cried out, she placed her hand over his mouth, shook her head, and whispered, "Hallway traffic. We have eight noiseless minutes to reach and respond to orgasm; eight minutes to shower and dress. The clock starts now."

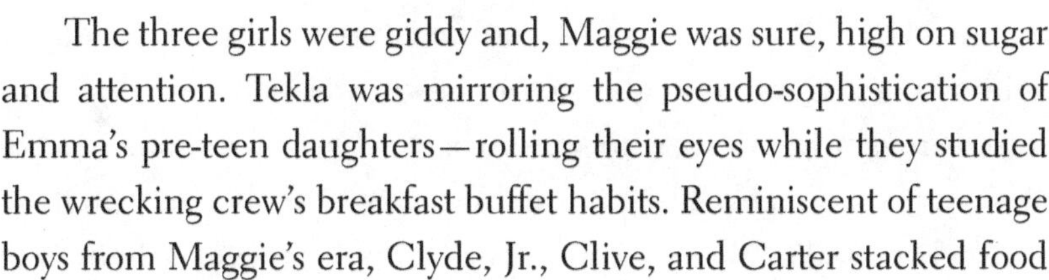

The three girls were giddy and, Maggie was sure, high on sugar and attention. Tekla was mirroring the pseudo-sophistication of Emma's pre-teen daughters—rolling their eyes while they studied the wrecking crew's breakfast buffet habits. Reminiscent of teenage boys from Maggie's era, Clyde, Jr., Clive, and Carter stacked food on their plates as if it was more logical to eat in layers.

Across the room, Jo seemed to be taking it all in with a hunger she'd always deprived. Dressed in black—a pair of Katherine Hepburn styled man-pants and turtleneck—her hair was freshly shampooed and pulled in a loose ponytail with a leopard-print scarf.

Maggie waved to Jo and pointed at two empty chairs as Jacques made his way to the front of the buffet line and cried, "*Bonjour! Puis-je avoir votre attention s'il vous plait?* Ah, good! You're all beginning to pick up a little French. Before we get lost in this wonderful meal, I'd like our inspired master chefs, Danielle, Sarah and Tekla, and their adult tag-team, Emma and Charles, to join me. Today we'll eat well and dig deep. This morning the girls decided to donate all their tips to The Hunger Project."

Smiling in blueberry-stained aprons, the five held hands and bowed several times during the prolonged whistleblowing, stomping and cheering. Maggie watched Tekla radiate energy and imagined some implicit oath to take better care of this tattered planet.

After she and Jo had chased their last pieces of French toast through small talk and blue-stained maple syrup, Jo looked at Maggie. Maggie looked back. Jo kept peering at her as if waiting for her to say something. Maggie finally put her coffee cup down and whispered, "What's going on? You okay?"

Jo smiled and said, "I'm very okay and proud of you and this remarkable girl who drew two of the best parents she could find. Having this coming-out party was never part of the bargain. I'm terrified about revealing myself, accounting for all the lies when we lived together. And, dear god, explaining why I gave you to Anna when I knew Raymond was a certified lunatic. Day after day, I rubbed my fingers along glass rosary beads; week after week, I confessed my sin to priests who were whacked by my tedious misery. Well, not every week. There were times when I took mercy on their dreary lives and made up some impure thoughts to cheer them up!" laughed Jo. "Maggie, I have no right to ask or expect your time or attention, but I so want the experience of being your mother, Sam's mother-in-law, Tekla's grandmother."

Maggie kissed Jo's cheek and said, "It's okay, Mom Jo. I've been looking for you my entire life and there's no way you're going to get away from me again. We've both suffered. When Tekla wants to celebrate or rail against her non-conformist, kickass families of origin or not-of-origin, I want her to know who they are, who you are! What we call you is your choice."

"Momjo? It has a nice island beat and you can dance to it," said Jo.

Maggie laughed, and said, "Oh, yeah, we be jukin' on da' island Momjo!"

After the boys took off for the Maple Leaf, and the cooking staff moved to the kitchen to wash dishes, Jacques stood up and said, "Before we head back to our rooms, Catherine and I want to share our sledgehammer wisdom. At some point during our sleepless night, we realized we were trying to 'reconstruct our new world' in less than twenty-four hours after spending a lifetime trying to keep our lies straight. We've obviously lost our minds and forgot how life works. Most sane, honest, thoughtful people know futures aren't static—they live, breathe, and move in directions we can't imagine. So, rather than attempt to read tea leaves and design tools for an unpredictable future, we thought we'd spend today filling in the blanks—answering questions about where we've been, what we've accomplished, and disclosing any existing or anticipated threats and promises. Issie?"

"Um. Sorry. Never mind."

"Two questions," said Blanche. "Adults only? And what's our schedule?"

"Yes, adults only. If anyone needs to head back home or is concerned about sitting in," said Catherine, "please let me know. Attendance isn't mandatory. We'd rather each person decide for him or herself. We'll begin at high noon."

Issie hung back as others left the room. Catherine waited.

"Um. Sorry. I didn't know how to say it out loud and thought I'd wait to talk to you alone."

"Sure, Issie. I'm glad you did."

"Huh. I'm having a hard time seeing you as Anna. Here I am, talking to my mother!" Issie's laugh was thin, stressed by her right heel jackhammering the floor.

"It's okay, Issie, go on."

"You know, it just seems impossible that I'm here and we're talking. I want to stay and talk more, but I can't. My husband Eddie is a line-worker at Ford, a UAW guy. A long time ago he got nailed as a snitch for blowing the whistle on one of his union brothers.

He's been looking over his shoulder ever since. Um . . . when I said I was going to Toronto to tell Maggie the truth about what I knew, Eddie said if I ever got mixed up with Oz, or any other communist organization, he'd take the boys and I'd never see him or them again.

"You see, Eddie used to be the nicest, funniest guy, but he's still taking his licks from the union. Then, we took a big hit when we had to sell off Egg On the Run to avoid bankruptcy. Seriously, he was knocked on his ass when that happened. It was my fault because I encouraged him and offered to run the business. What a mess. I didn't know anything about running a business and I almost put us . . ." Issie looked around as if she'd rather be anywhere else. Then, looked at Catherine before she realized she was in the middle of a sentence. "Anyhow, I'm pretty sure Oz isn't a communist organization, but Eddie's one of those 'rather be dead than red' Americans. He thinks everything that isn't made in the USA—or any car not built by the UAW—is because of communism. I can't push him right now. As much as I want to, I can't stay."

Catherine put her arms around Issie and held her tight. "Oh, Issie, my beautiful, Issie Belle. How hard this must have been for you as the big sister, then young wife, and now mother. There aren't enough ways to let you know how sorry I am that I didn't show up for you when you needed me." Stepping back, with her hands on Issie's shoulders, Catherine said, "I want you to hear me say this. It's not a criticism of you or Eddie or anyone else. I know that we sometimes recreate the relationship our parents modeled for us. You just told me you try to manage Eddie's anger by avoiding the hot spots. I did that far too many years and almost self-destructed. I can help you with support, money, advice—whatever you need to build a healthier relationship or reach a decision to separate. I have no idea if Eddie is like Raymond, but I spent too much time dealing with Raymond's crazy, controlling behavior to keep my mouth shut. After today, you and I will talk, we'll visit. I want to get to know you, my grandsons and Eddie. But promise me this—if you ever feel a threat of any kind for any reason—you will damn-well call me. If Eddie hits you or threatens to hit you, you will take the boys and leave. You have my private number. I can be reached anywhere at any time. Issie Belle, I want you to promise."

Studying Catherine's eyes, Issie was transported through the change of seasons, years and decades—warping time, place and age. Yet her eyes were the same, Anna's eyes. Issie nodded.

When Catherine walked into the meeting room, Maggie, Sam, Clyde, Blanche, Loretta, and Jo had formed a circle.

"Issie decided to opt-out," said Catherine. "She wanted to stay but decided Eddie and the boys needed her at home. Without going into detail, I'm sure she'd be fine if I told you that Eddie doesn't trust foreign organizations like Oz because they might be connected to communist regimes. According to Issie, Eddie's loyalty is reserved for his family, his country, the UAW and Ford."

"I'd add the Detroit Tigers and Domino's Pizza to his list," laughed Sam. "But the dude has this unbelievable capacity to imagine and invent. He's like an Einstein in steel-toed work boots."

"Yes!" said Maggie. "The Einstein side of him is amazing. Every invention feels like a ride on *La Coquette*."

"Help me," said Clyde, "*La Coquette?*"

"Philias Fogg's gas balloon in *Around the World in 80 Days*."

Just then, Jacques wheeled a mobile corkboard through the door and rattled it across the floor. On the front side, someone had tacked their names along the top of the board; thumbtacks lined both sides. Catherine removed Issie's name, then took a small index card and tacked it below Maggie's name. She had everyone's attention.

Still looking at the board, Catherine said, "I posted a question for Maggie. I have questions for others that I'll add, but for now,

I want to give you a preview of how we think this will work. My question is: If you can only ask one more question about your childhood, what would it be? Not very original, but we're dealing with time constraints and it might push us to . . .

Mercifully, Jacques tapped Catherine's shoulder and shook his head no. When she looked behind her, she saw a living tableau of aghast, wide-eyed, Picasso-inspired expressions, then doubled over in laughter. "Or not!" she cried. "Let's keep the cards, ditch the corkboard and let 'er rip."

Maggie listened to the rush of pencils flying through words. The sound would normally jumpstart her adrenalin. But not today.

# 24

# Attractive Nuisances

FRIDAY AFTERNOON, SEPTEMBER 23, 1977—Listening to index cards being sorted and shuffled, Maggie was swept back in time to Aunt Minnie's Bridge games in the parlor—a room filled with travel books, quirky little knickknacks, and souvenirs. As a child, Maggie thought it the most touchable room in the house; yet it was the only room with a no-touch rule.

Before Maggie could pronounce the word prohibition, she knew it made things more attractive. Don't climb the tree, walk up the downside of the slide, or talk in the library. When faced with these kinds of bans, it seemed impossible to shake off the idea of revolt. With all the broken rules littering her mind, Maggie found the metaphysical landing in Aunt Minnie's parlor an absurd stretch.

After a few minutes of sorting, discarding, and choosing the order of their questions, Jacques asked Maggie to begin. The air in the room seemed to lift as shoulders relaxed.

With no index card, Maggie looked at Jacques and asked, "Why did you choose Oz over marriage, family, friends, and tranquility?"

"My short answer is I didn't choose Oz over marriage or family or friends. As to tranquility, it was never in the mix; and, by my standards, highly overrated.

"Oz chose me after I was tossed in the slammer for inciting a riot. I wasn't inciting a riot. I was vigorously protesting the Padlock Act in Quebec, circa 1937. With the ink still wet on my master's in fine arts, and still wearing my black graduation gown, I wrapped a heavy chain and padlock around my neck. I didn't know much about civil disobedience, but I was outraged. I stood on a park bench in Quebec's Place Royale Square, near the statue of King Louis XIV, and began my ad hoc 'give me free speech or give me death' diatribe. Back then, the Padlock Act gave deputized pissants the authority to padlock doors when the meetings held behind those doors threatened the 'common good.' The Act was intended to make it illegal for communists to gather, meet, and form alliances. But like most prohibitions based on non-majority beliefs, the Act was weaponized to harass Jews, unionists, the political left . . . outsiders. Fresh turbulence at a time when Oz was beginning to blow the whistle on the United Kingdom for their history of atrocities against humankind.

"You won't read about Britain's atrocities in history books. In the Anglo-Boar War, at the turn of the century, Lord Horatio Kitchener led the British army in the scorched-earth slaughter of livestock and torching of homesteads to flush out guerillas. Success was measured by the weekly 'bag' of killed, captured, and wounded.

"More than one hundred and fifty thousand men, women and children were forcibly moved into the first concentration camps built by a European nation. Not under a despotic German Kaiser, but under Great Britain's regal Queen Victoria.

"Across South Africa, almost thirty-thousand white Boer women and children, and twenty-five thousand black Africans, were killed by neglect or force. According to historians and human rights organizations, Britain's total 'bag of killed' was at best an estimate because it either took too much time to count, or the lives of these foreign men, women and children didn't count.

"Children fared the worst. I hope to never forget the photograph of Lizzie van Zvi, an emaciated eleven-year-old Boer girl dying on a cot. Because Lizzie's mother was an 'undesirable,' and her father refused to surrender, her rations were reduced. Because she didn't speak English, Lizzie was treated like an idiot. Her cries ignored. Lizzie died on that cot. For what? You see, South Africa was a treasure trove of gold and diamonds.

"You won't read about Britain's crimes against humanity in your history books. You'll find marching bands, waving flags and Lord Horatio Kitchener's likeness plastered across World War One army recruitment posters. You might feel a sense of pride when you learn the city of Berlin, Ontario decided to change its name because of anti-German sentiments. Lord Kitchener's death, a few weeks before the vote, led to the spoils. Berlin, Ontario was renamed Kitchener, Ontario. Poetic justice or the power of propaganda?

"Because we call ourselves civilized, doesn't mean we're civilized. When we padlock—shut down, incarcerate, starve, or incinerate human beings who don't share our world view—we're not civilized. Conquests are not a badge of honor or privilege, they are crimes. Ask India.

"Yet, Buckingham Palace—with its gilded carriages, ceremonial queen, and preening royalty—continues to provide cover for the money brokers, deal makers and political carpetbaggers. You need money and connections to sustain this twentieth-century charade. How much? The shadow of Buckingham Palace literally falls on squatters—the Brit's pejorative for people so poor they sleep on cardboard and beg for food.

"Oz chose me after my amateur *pièce de resistance*; before I had the chance to choose them. So here we are in 1977, with 'civilized' nations still imposing their privilege and trampling the rights of the conquered, the occupied, the oppressed. Follow the spoils.

"And Oz. Why didn't we blow the whistle on the juicers sooner? Did we think we were better, incorruptible? We proved ourselves wrong. Power hijacked our egos. If we can't get out of our own way, we're doomed."

There was a brooding pause before Clyde said, "I'll go next. Although there are deeper, more important questions, I have no doubt my question for Sam will get a lot of press." Reading from his index card, Clyde said, "My three-part question is: Were you the subject of gaslighting, drugs, and video sex? If so, do you know who entrapped you? And how will you handle questions from the press?"

Nodding his head, Sam looked around the room before he said, "Maggie knows about these escapades with other women. I let her believe I was the victim. And I was the intended victim. The mob and juicers wanted to set me up. When Maggie, Clyde and I talked about it, we knew who the bad guys were. What Maggie and Clyde didn't know was Oz helped pull this off and I was actively involved.

"The women who worked for the mob were Oz operatives—double agents—and the nudity and touching between us was mostly smoke, mirrors and camera angles. I knew to play along as if I was drugged. I was so freaked by the assignments that it was hard to act like I felt pleasure. We had to convince the bad guys they 'owned' me.

"Looking at Maggie's face right now, I wish there'd been a good time to bring this up—a better time to confess a lie. To be clear, I knew both women were Oz operatives and double agents. I knew the mob wanted to buy my loyalty in the juicing operation. And I knew Oz wanted to safeguard my status as an operative.

"There was no way to really know these women. Both used aliases, showed up, then disappeared. Back then, I didn't know if Clyde was in on it and couldn't ask. My job was to keep it real—which meant I told Clyde and Maggie about my encounters and helped them conclude I was being drugged and gaslighted. That's it."

"Are you effing kidding me?" said Maggie. "You knew and you let me think you were doing drugs, seducing women and . . . what? . . . getting off on group sex?"

"Mag, I knew, but I couldn't tell you. As we just found out, the stakes were high enough to fake a plane crash and abduct Tekla and me in broad daylight. For all this time I was a wreck because I had to lie to you. To nail the juicers, I had to act like I was high on drugs and pretend to jackoff in seedy skin-flicks. Maggie, I swear, there was no way I could tell you the truth until Oz released the documents."

All eyes were on Maggie as she began to nod—mentally checking off each conversation, argument, promise and lie that led to Sam's confession. Sam didn't move. No one moved until Maggie said, "Okay."

"Whew! Now I get why Maggie was freaked out about you having affairs with other women," said Loretta. "I thought she just had too much time on her hands."

"I did have too much time on my hands," said Maggie. "This trip was going to lead me to be the activist I never was. Now, I'm thinking PTA."

"Please, god," said Blanche. "On your first solo activist venture, you flipped the international crime syndicate on its ass. I say pitch your cookie sheets and calling trees. You're way too dangerous for the PTA."

"Amen to that," said Loretta.

"Amen is right," said Sam.

"Yep," said Maggie, "I can almost see the mobsters shaking in their sharkskin suits."

"And so they should!" said Catherine. "Other questions before we take a break?"

Although Maggie understood the questions were mostly for her benefit, her mind wandered. Everyone seemed over-animated—as if they wanted to force-feed her energy. Instead, she felt some kind of agitated-tranquility. No doubt triggered by Jacques' slur about tranquility, Maggie realized the agitation side of the equation wasn't because of Sam's lies; it was provoked by the amount of time they were spending on the past rather than the present.

"Maggie," said Catherine, "are you ready with a question?"

"Oddly, no. For some reason, I keep drifting off. At first, I thought it was environmental—too much food, too little fresh air, no movement. But then it hit me. We're stuck in the past instead of experiencing the present. Crazy isn't it? I'm seriously torqued by this state-of-mind shift. After twenty years of pushing, insisting, and pitching fits to induce this watershed moment, I'm suddenly clamoring for the present."

Wide-eyed and quiet, everyone looked confused. Maggie nodded and said, "Okay, I got it. Crazy is as crazy does. Tapping into that, I have a question. Does anyone know if I ever had a *Twilight Zone* kind of thing in Aunt Minnie's parlor when I was about six or seven?"

"Where did that come from?" asked Jo.

"When we were shuffling index cards, the sound reminded me of Minnie's Bridge games—which led me to that whimsical room and my unbearable temptation to touch every untouchable object."

Jo's eyes turned up—as if searching her collective unconscious—before she said, "When Minnie and Cyp couldn't conceive children, it took years for her to make peace with a barren womb and empty rooms. An ideal setting for two sisters who had sex with reckless men, popped out babies and left them for Minnie to raise for thirteen-plus years. Under all her bluster, Minnie knew how to give shelter and express love. Kindness was a little tricky, but she knew when to call on her saints and, trust me, Minnie knew which saints to call.

"Because the two of you were Minnie's only chance to be a mother, she learned to take pleasure in complaining about Elvis shaking the rafters—or pretending to bang her head against the wall when you showed up in a wrinkled uniform or sagging knee socks. She'd watched other mothers. But Minnie didn't need help when it came to bragging rights. It only took an audience of one for her to bend ears about her girls flying through catechism, nursing wounded birds, winning spelling bees.

"The only parlor-room story I remember about you, Maggie, was the day Minnie found you on the floor with a box of old photos. You were looking at the picture of a very pregnant me a few days before you were born. Because we'd avoided photos of me from the waist down, I was sure Minnie wanted that photo as evidence of my sin, and I knew I deserved it.

"Minnie said she watched you humming and smiling at that photo for the longest time before you kissed it and tucked it in your pocket. Then, you placed the lid on the box of photos and returned it to the bottom shelf of the bookcase. When you looked up and saw Minnie at the door, she saw the terror in your eyes. Instead of scolding you, the saints kicked in. Minnie told me she blinked back tears, smiled, and said, 'Any chance you want to go to Kresge's to spin around on the big red stools and share a Tin Roof?' And you, my love, said, 'Is the pope Catholic?'"

# 25

# Zoo Day

SUNDAY, AUGUST 3, 1980—Tekla knew her life was totally weird. Three years ago, after they made it home from the fake-plane-crash-that-no-one-wants-to-talk-about, Sam decided to become a pioneer househusband so Maggie could teach and write poetry. Before Maggie had time to look for a job, Sam lost his job, and they all moved into a bigger house. A few months later, the *Detroit Free Press* stopped by to do a complete spread on the 'Modern Family.'

*Time to face facts,* thought Tekla. Her parents, relatives and their friends were complete oddballs. They spoke different languages, had different skin colors, ate different kinds of food. To mix it up, her Uncle Kenny and Aunt Stella were an Oreo couple—Uncle Kenny was pure white, Aunt Stella was pure black. As if that wasn't enough, Tekla had always called her parents by their first names. For years it was no big deal, but after her eleventh birthday, everything changed because everything was a big deal. Tekla started to collect all the reasons she was an outsider and pinned them in her scrapbook brain like dead butterflies.

Tekla was sure no one else had an Oreo couple in their family; the kids at school acted like it was something you saw at a freak show. Then, when Tekla talked about her black aunts and uncles, the kids mocked her. Some smart-aleck sixth-grader said Tekla was probably an albino-negro, which caught on until the new principal, Mr. Goodfriend, told everyone there was no such thing as an albino-negro. To make matters worse, Maggie spoke with a French accent. Tekla begged her not to talk, but Maggie would laugh and tell Tekla to get over herself. Although Tekla had no idea what that meant, the issue soon became her first existential nightmare—who was she?

Uncle Willie's Zoo Day was the first Sunday of every August—Tekla's favorite day of the year until she started her twelfth revolution around the sun.

"Hey, Moonwalker! You dressed? We're meeting Uncle Clyde and Aunt Blanche for breakfast before we head to the zoo," called Maggie.

"Not going and stop calling me Moonwalker."

"What do you mean you're not going? I thought you loved Zoo Day."

"I'm not a baby."

"No, you're not, so why are you acting like one?"

Sitting at the end of her bed—dressed in a faded Princess Leia nightie, knees to her chin, mousey-brown hair standing on end—Tekla's mouth snarled into a pout.

"Okay, Tekla, if you don't want to go, I'll call a sitter."

"I told you I'm not a baby. I don't need a sitter."

"A sitter or the zoo. Your choice."

"How about Grandma Tervo?"

"Nope. She and Uncle Pete are heading to Mackinaw. Sitter or Zoo? Decide now or I'll decide for you."

"Is the wrecking crew going? I don't want to be the only kid."

"Clyde Junior and Clive are helping Uncle Willie set up the picnic area at the zoo; they'll be grilling hot dogs and hamburgers all day. Carter's meeting us for breakfast."

Tekla worked hard not to smile and said, "Okay. If Carter's there, I'll go. But I'm not spending the whole stupid day with stupid adults."

"Got it. You might want to work on synonyms for stupid. Carter's fourteen and I'm sure he's into three-syllable words."

When Maggie and Sam narced Tekla out of her bratty behavior, it cheered her up. She felt loved when they called her bluff. Plus, it was hard for her to keep up the act. Tekla wanted to go to Zoo Day and hang out with her crazy aunts and uncles—even her hippity-do-da parents—but thought it'd be nice if someone asked. Tekla supposed Uncle Kenny and Aunt Stella were still in Paris doing their Oreo Tour for the book they wrote. *Oh, cripes!* she thought. *That's all I need, more bad press.*

By the time the Tervos got to Big Boys, the Websters were seated in a large booth.

"Hey, Moonwalker," called Uncle Clyde. "Still dragging around those two butt-ugly, cranky parents?"

"Hey, Uncle Clyde! I know. I keep trying to lose them, but nothing works," said Tekla, before she twisted both her fists in front of her eyes and turned down her mouth like she was crying.

After giving Aunt Blanche a quick hug, Tekla slid into the booth next to Carter who was reading a yellowed copy of *The Invisible Man*.

"Good book?" she asked.

Carter looked at her like she was from another planet and said, "I guess."

"What's it about?"

"Being invisible."

"What?"

"About being black in a white world. About being invisible."

"Who's invisible?"

Carter gave her the you-ditz look and shook his head. "Never mind. You're too young. I'll tell you about it when you're older."

Tears started to form in Tekla's eyes, and she bit them back with an anger that almost knocked her over, and whispered, "Screw you, Carter Webster. You might be a few years older, but you don't know your ass from a . . . stupid . . . bowling ball."

Carter closed his book before he turned to look at Tekla. With soft brown skin like Uncle Clyde, and hazel eyes flecked by gold and green, Tekla wanted to disappear in that universe. Before she could find words, Carter nodded his head and said, "I'm sorry I blew you off. Your question makes sense; my response didn't."

Sam looked over and said, "Hey, you two, listen up. Clyde has an announcement to make. Drum roll please!"

Clyde stood, bent at the waist, then sat back down. *Cripes,* thought Tekla, *why can't they just act normal out in public?*

"Let me remind you that nine-plus years ago the General Manager of the Red Wings fired Willie from his job as the Zamboni Driver. Willie worked there almost twenty years until the nineteen-year-old nephew of the Wing's biggest sponsor got the urge to drive a Zamboni. Willie not only lost his job; he lost his Mr. Zamboni gig and just about lost his self-respect. But there were forces of good at work. Before a week passed, the G.M. who fired Willie got fired. Willie was offered the choice of getting his job back or helping the Wings put together a program to open the Detroit Zoo to kids with parents who couldn't take them to the zoo because they were poor or in jail. Willie chose the kids. Since then, Zoo Day has expanded its reach to include the care and preservation of animals all over the world. Today, Willie will announce new funding to provide scholarships for minority students who want to become veterinarians."

"Screw minority," Carter whispered under his breath.

"What's wrong with minority?" Tekla whispered back.

Carter looked at her and shook his head. "You're white, you don't get it, and you won't ever get it."

"Try me."

Carter shook his head and opened his book.

Tekla was sure she was the only kid who didn't have a tribe. Not black, not Christian, not Catholic, not Jewish—not Mexican, Italian, or Polish. A freaking middle-class mongrel and outcast. An encyclopedia of dead butterflies.

The zoo was packed. Maggie thought the animals must be thrilled by so many vibrant creatures stopping to talk in those high-pitched falsetto voices people use when they talk to four-legged mammals and winged species. The reptiles and amphibians get the lower ranges. And, with all the bright straw hats, swinging skirts and boisterous sun umbrellas, Maggie was sure the opulent birds were checking out the competition.

After waiting in long food lines, shortened by conversation and laughter, the humans were fed and invited to sit in the tent-shaded outdoor auditorium. Without introduction, Willie walked onto the small stage and waved to the audience before he pulled up a stool and lowered the microphone. The fingernails-on-a-chalkboard screech from the mic raised jeers from the birdhouse, prompted a thirty-yard dash by the flamingos, and set off the chimpanzees. The crowd cheered and Willie's smile reached the back row.

"Happy Zoo Day!" cried Willie. "For those of you I haven't met, my name is Willie Johnson. I've got the best job in the world.

"For those of you who know me and have heard about my first trip to the zoo a dozen times, I beg your indulgence. You see these gray hairs? I'm old and tend to repeat myself. But on Zoo Day, I repeat this story to honor Mavis Johnson, my ma. I wouldn't be on this extraordinary adventure if she hadn't broken all the color barriers to take me here when I was six years old. Imagine the courage it took forty years ago for a skinny, young black girl to dress in her Sunday best and take her six-year-old son on the Detroit Metro bus and get off at Ten Mile in Royal Oak? Now, think about the audacity she must have had to line up with all those white folks and buy tickets to the zoo. Most of you are too far away to see these blue eyes in my black face. You see, Ma was only twelve when I was born . . . with blue eyes . . . in the deep south." Willie waited for stillness to set in before he said, "My guess is none of you need a playbill.

"During the Second World War money was tight and food was scarce. I don't know what it cost for two people to take the bus and get into the zoo, but it took Ma weeks to save fifty cents for our zoo day. To say I was over the moon when I saw my first giraffe is a bold-faced . . . understatement. I literally flew to the fence to get a closer look. I was so excited I missed clearing a little white girl in a pink dress holding an ice cream cone. When she fell and lost her ice cream, she started bawling. Her father snatched me by my skinny arm and tossed me across the green space onto the sidewalk. His words are indelible, 'You two black sambos belong in a cage. Get the hell out of here and stay out!' My ma and I were both crying when she took my hand. She was so small people must have thought we were both kids. As we walked out of the zoo everyone stood stock-still and stared at us as if we were aliens. Across the Atlantic, Germany was designing the perfect race. Yet, everyone stood stock-still. No one said a word. Ma was only eighteen. It was her first and only visit to the zoo.

"Today we still battle racism, but not at the zoo. At the zoo, we're making important strides in raising the awareness of both human and animal rights. Animals are being treated with more respect, their habitats more natural, open, and friendly. People of every race, nationality and color are invited to the table and hired to promote our good work . . . "

Maggie's attention wandered as Willie talked about each of the initiatives the zoo was taking . . . the new species of animals they were adding . . .. When she heard Willie say 'giraffe,' she tuned back in.

"The giraffe's still my favorite animal for all the obvious psycho-social reasons—my first love and trailblazer. To be sure, I've got the best job there is. But it costs money to keep these beautiful animals safe from predators and extinction, to give them the space, food and care they deserve. In the packet of information under your chair, you'll find plans for developing better habitats and providing scholarships for minorities interested in veterinary medicine. I'm not going to take time to twist arms, I'm sure the materials and ideas speak for themselves. I only ask that you review this information and send us a check. Fifty cents is the minimum, there is no maximum. I'll hang around for questions, comments or an analysis of the Red Wings' chances for the Stanley Cup."

Willie was always good at basking in the applause; he admitted it was what he liked best about being Mr. Zamboni. And, once again, his smile reached the back row. Maggie knew Willie was a take-no-prisoners kind of guy. He never gave up. But, until today, she never fully understood Willie's power to inspire—or his energy to create, promote and change the world.

By five o'clock the zoo was almost empty. Hooked on the show *Little House on the Prairie*, Tekla knew the menfolk would clean up the picnic area and shut down the barbeque pits while the womenfolk gathered somewhere else. Turned out to be near the zoo entrance. Tekla stretched out on one of the benches and pretended sleep. Before long, Momjo lifted Tekla's head, sat down, and began petting her hair. Tekla sighed and decided being the baby wasn't all bad.

"Each year I think it can't get better and it does. Who knew Willie would channel his little boy spirit and turn this into an international event!" said Jo.

Willie's wife, Robin, in a yellow-flowered sundress, with a matching fabric belt and yellow straw hat, said, "Lord, god, that man of mine needed a miracle and god delivered."

"I never understood why you and Willie decided not to have babies. You're both so good with kids," said Maggie.

Tekla squinted through narrow eye-slits and watched Aunt Robin shift on the bench, then brush out the folds in her dress before she looked at Maggie and said, "No way was Willie going to bring a black baby into this broken world. He knows their chance of getting locked up is way better than their chance of going to college. And he knows all too well what it's like to be invisible."

"Amen to that," said Blanche. "Who's minding the revolving door at criminal court?"

Taking off her straw hat and fanning her face, Robin said, "Willie about killed himself doing both jobs before he decided it made more sense to help kids before they get in trouble. This year he finally turned over his watchdog work to a young man from Tuskegee who wants to be a civil rights leader. Imagine, educated, ambitious young men who want to fight the system. Sometimes I forget there are others out there kicking the dirt, willing to work for a cause instead of a paycheck. Two days later, some lawyer, named Bruce Shelton, called Willie out of the blue and asked him to serve on a nationwide criminal oversight board. Only meets four times a year; plus, they pay for his hotel and travel expenses!"

Loretta did her fist-pumping thing without jumping up, and said, "Lord almighty! Willie's changing the world and making a name for himself."

"About time. Willie's worked his butt off; he deserves it," said Blanche.

Then there was silence. Tekla propped herself up on her elbow to see what was going on. The womenfolk were watching the menfolk walk down the wide sidewalk carrying picnic baskets, cardboard boxes, bags of charcoal and ice chests. All black and brown faces except for Sam. Like a locomotive full of masculine energy—talking, joking, laughing—generous, good-looking men and almost-men. Tekla felt a shiver move up her spine and flashed onto the idea that people might be better off choosing their tribes than getting stuck with one they don't like.

# 26

# Isms

MONDAY, AUGUST 4, 1980—"Okay, Tekla. Because you're finally eleven, you're entitled to 'Three Issie-Isms to Live By.' Listen up! These isms will keep you sane when you're sure no one else is."

"Aunt Issie, please no. I don't know what an ism is, but if it's one of those 'you're a young lady now' lectures about men-stir-a-tion, Kotex and boys, I got it."

Tekla watched Issie do that torque-thing she does—drumming her feet against the floor like a wild banshee and shaking her head back and forth before she finally cracks up. "Oh my god, Tekla, you're a trip! I promise this is not a lecture about men-stir-a-tion, Kotex or boys. This is your crazy Aunt Issie's worldview. Ready?"

Tekla wasn't ready but she knew turning down Aunt Issie was like trying to stay up on a fast-rolling log in Lake Michigan. No way it's going to happen. Besides being Maggie's big sister and only sib, Aunt Issie was the funniest grown-up Tekla knew. Issie's code word for advice was 'spare change.' Whenever Tekla wanted to complain about Maggie, Sam, or her dumb life, she called Aunt Issie.

Tekla gave Issie her brattiest 'take-no-prisoners evil eye' before she smiled and said, "Sure, Aunt Iss, I could use some spare change."

Returning her evil eye, Issie began. "First, absurdism. This is a mind-blowing, irrational universe. Do not think for a solitary minute that you can outguess, outsmart or out-maneuver everything that comes your way. Won't happen. You'll get blindsided, cheated, knocked on your ass. Once you know this, you'll stop freaking out every time your feelings get hurt or you skin your knee. Just let it be and say to yourself, 'this is absurdism in action.' Got it?"

"Aunt Issie, are you sure I need to hear all three at one time?"

"Absurdism, Moonwalker—whoops, sorry, I mean Tekla. Next ism, deism. Believe in god but—hear me say this—reject religion. Religion is big business. The Catholic Church makes General Motors look like a lemonade stand. No shit, Tekla. They build these gigantic cathedrals on the backs of poor people. Beware—there's no one right way to be in this world. Just because a bunch of old dudes with long beards thought they had it all figured out a thousand years ago doesn't cut it. These desert cowboys also thought men were smarter than women. We know that's total bullshit."

By then, Tekla was lost in what Sam calls 'pure Issie.'

"And the third and most important ism is optimism. In spite of all the crazy shit that goes on, we live in the best possible world. So, my sweet, sassy Tekla Tervo, hold onto optimism. No matter how bad, sad, or angry you feel, there's always a new day rolling your way, ready to call your name. This isn't about magic or luck, it's about the choices we make. You already know how to be bold and kick ass, to be serious and get your work done. Now it's time to practice optimism—happiness, joy, whatever you want to call it. It too is an option, a matter of choice."

"I like the last ism, but the other two sound bogus."

"Bogus? No kidding? Do you even know what that means?"

"Like fake, untrue."

"Cool! You're listening, taking it in and making decisions for yourself. Those are my isms, Tekla. You'll find your own, and I hope, optimism makes your shortlist."

"Aunt Iss, did your divorce make you happy?"

"Not at first. I missed the idea of family-life—big Thanksgiving dinners, Christmas carols, family reunions. But those ideas turned out to be mind-farts, too many Hallmark Card commercials and *Look* magazine covers. Eddie and I never had the made-for-TV family-life and it sure as hell wasn't like that when I was a kid.

"After the divorce, I decided to get my head on straight: grow up; act like an adult; make decisions; pay bills; keep up with the chores; help the boys with homework—not! I don't help the boys with homework, but they do help me act like an adult. Scary stuff being a grown-up after a forty-year childhood," laughed Issie.

"Are you still mad at Eddie?"

"Sometimes. When I'm tired or overwhelmed, I blame everything on Eddie because I can."

Tekla looked down and began picking at the nubby fabric on the sofa. Without looking up, she said, "Sometimes I curl up in a ball under my covers and pretend I'm a caterpillar. But it's really boring."

"What a great idea! But why a caterpillar?"

"Duh. Because a caterpillar becomes a butterfly."

Pretending she had a microphone in her hand, Issie reached out and said, "And why, Miss Tervo, do you want to become a butterfly?"

Tekla tightened her fists and attempted an evil eye, but tears flowed when Tekla said, "Because . . . because I don't want Maggie and Sam to get a divorce."

"Of course, you don't. Why do you think they will?"

"You promise not to tell?"

"As long as not-telling doesn't hurt anyone, I promise."

Issie could almost see Tekla mentally rehearsing what she wanted to say before she said, "Okay. Maggie and Grandma Tervo were talking, and Grandma Tervo said, 'Praise the lord that sister of yours finally got divorced;' and Maggie said real loud, 'It was about damn time! Thank god she's on her own!'"

Suppressing a smile, Issie said, "Hmm. I can see why you're a little freaked out. Listening to those words, it sounds like divorce is the best thing to do. Is that what you thought?"

Tekla nodded.

"Okay. Because I talked with your Grandma Tervo and Maggie before I got divorced, I hear something different. What I hear is their relief because I'm happier. For sure, marriage has its ups and downs. Eddie, me, and the boys have a ton of super-good, far-out memories—building Eddie's wild-ass inventions; bingeing popcorn on the roof of our old Galaxy at the drive-in; playing baseball with sticks, spatulas, croquet mallets, whatever! When things got bad, we tried as hard as we could to keep our family together. But we couldn't. Divorce wasn't an easy choice, but for each of us, it was the best choice. And, get this, Eddie's ready to walk down the aisle again."

"Holy crap!" said Tekla.

"Does Maggie know you talk like a sailor?"

"Does everyone know you and Maggie talk like sailors?"

"No shit," laughed Issie, "it must run in the family."

"Hey, Moonwalker, how was your day at Issie's new townhouse?"

"Ugh! You promised to call me Tekla."

"Okay, then. Hey, Tekla, how was your day at Issie's new townhouse?"

"You don't have to make fun of me because I want you to call me by the name YOU gave me."

"Tekla, I'm not making fun of you. Did you and Issie have a bad day?"

After scorching Maggie with her meanest evil eye, Tekla stomped off to her bedroom.

Maggie sat down in the kitchen and looked around. When they returned from their watershed reunion in Toronto almost three years ago, they found a job termination and eviction notice nailed to their front door. Sam's termination from Jingo Motors as Director of Personnel was effective immediately; the eviction notice gave them two weeks to vacate the property. The house, mortgaged by Jingo Motors, was under their payroll-deduction plan. There would be no payoffs or reimbursements under either notice; and Jingo made it clear they would not provide references to future landlords, mortgagers, or employers.

Maggie and Sam took turns being pissed-off so one of them could keep their game face while they checked the house and tucked in Tekla and Windsor Dog. Then, Sam put a Bee Gee's album on the stereo and turned "Staying Alive" up to 'barely audible' before he began shaking his hips and lip-syncing the words. Before they both lost control with soundless giggles, flying arms, body bumps and shimmies. When they stopped, they hugged and cried before they talked and talked. By sunrise, they'd crafted a plan and a back-up plan. It felt like a toehold on sanity.

When they called Jacques, he told them to find a four-bedroom house with two baths within walking distance to Tekla's school and he'd take care of the rest. Three days later they found a three-bedroom house with a den and two baths on Munger, a few country blocks from the school. Backing up to a ravine, the property included a small stable for horses, dogs, or both. Tekla was over the moon.

After three years, Maggie was still smacked by awe. One of the few brick houses along that ragged east side of Livonia, most of their friends and neighbors thought they'd robbed a bank. Inside, they flopped on the same shabby-chic furniture, shag carpet, rag rugs, and wrestled books, games, and magazines out of the same misshapen wicker baskets. But the laundry room was a different story. Sam told anyone who'd listen that Maggie liked to pet the Harvest Gold top-loading washer and matching dryer and cry 'glory hallelujah!' Maggie would smile. Sam thought she was coveting the appliances. What she was coveting was her freedom from housework. She'd teach twelve hours a day for that pact.

With pennants from all over the world hanging from the ceiling, Tekla's room looked like an African casbah, a Roma camp, a colorful Turkish yurt. When Maggie walked in, Tekla was sitting at the end of her chain-hung bed, swinging it from side to side.

"Hey, Tekla, sorry I gave you a hard time. How's Aunt Issie?"

"Good. She made me listen to her Issie Isms."

"And?"

"And I like optimism."

"But not absurdism or deism?"

"You know?"

"Yep. You can't hang out with Issie without hearing about her isms."

"Do you have isms?"

"The boarding school we went to was a Petri dish for studying isms—racism, sexism, classism, nationalism—you name it. When you were little, Grandma Tervo used to shake her head back and forth, tsk twice, then whisper to her friends, 'Oy yoy yoy! My sweet Tekla's first drawing was on the back of a Free Angela Davis poster; she never had a chance.' You, my love, are infected by isms. I'm glad you had that talk with Issie."

"Uncle Eddie's going to walk down the aisle again. Yikes!"

"Yikes is right. Issie thought he might. I hoped he wouldn't."

"Why? Are you against marriage?"

"What? Why would I be against marriage? I'm married."

"Just asking."

# 27

# The Holy Grail

MONDAY EVENING, AUGUST 4, 1980—The master bedroom in the new house was twice as big as their old one—with a padded window seat for reading and its own bathroom. Sam called it The Ritz.

Another hot summer night, Maggie was stretched sideways across the bed in a pair of shorty pajamas. Sam was shedding his clothes after his daylong meeting with Oz. Maggie checked him out in his middle-aged blue boxer shorts and white tee shirt. He'd finally tossed his tighty whities.

"How was your meeting with Jacques and company?"

Sam pulled on Maggie's ankles to straighten her on the bed, then stretched out next to her. "There's a lot going on. Do you want the short version or the long version?"

"Long, please. It's too hot to sleep and I've been spending too much time with Emily Dickinson."

"New neighbor?"

"Very funny! Everyone has at least heard of Emily."

"If you say so."

"Seriously? You haven't heard of Emily?"

Sam had such an easy-to-spot shit-eating-grin. Maggie punched him in the shoulder and said, "Did you read Sound-Off in the *Free Press* today? Some guy complained about daylight savings time because . . . get this . . . he thinks the extra hour of sun after work means he has to mow his yard more often."

Sam looked at Maggie, popped open his eyes and said, "Damn-it-to-hell, woman! Are you telling me we have to change our clocks twice a year and we don't get that extra hour of promised sun?"

"You are such a guy," laughed Maggie.

"Okay, Mrs. Tervo, I need an update on your schedule and I'll update you on mine. Then, we need to talk about our relationship or non-relationship with Bruce."

Maggie reacted to Bruce's name with a loud sigh. She thought they'd finally buried her revenge affair with Bruce because of Sam's real or imagined escapades. But like her, Sam was a pit bull when it came to devising new plans or licking old wounds.

"Maggie, sigh all you want. But here's the rub, Oz hangs on the strength of relationships. That doesn't mean we have to like each other; it means we understand the risks and opportunities to accomplish goals far beyond our small selves. We need Bruce and Bruce needs us."

"Then let's talk about Bruce first and get him out of our bed."

"In that case, let's sit up."

After they sat up, Maggie took Sam's hand and said, "Sorry, babe, that was mean and bitchy. I'm here—ready for whatever conversation comes my way."

"Then let me build some scaffolding to give you context. This househusband cover story works for friends and neighbors; but the lynchpins and lobbyists in the food and meat-packing industries have their field glasses aimed at Oz and, we can assume, me. These guys make the juicers look like third stringers. Before the first saltine cracker, slice of cheese or ring bologna rode the assembly line, they were destined for adulteration. Nutrition was never the goal. As Jacques likes to say, follow the spoils. The mass production of food equals vast sums of money. We're talking heavy hitters."

"Sam, you're beginning to sound like a down-on-his-luck detective in a paperback novel. Do we need this much scaffolding?"

"Hang on. This is important. At the start of the century, Dr. Harvey Wiley was Chief Chemist at the U.S. Department of Agriculture. He's the mad scientist in this mystery. The 'Frankenstein' who conducted an absurd, off-the-wall experiment to test chemicals that kept food fresh from farm to factory to grocer to pantry. Wiley convinced the feds to give him money to recruit healthy young men—civil service clerks—to participate in his study. For five dollars per month and free meals, the 'Poison Squad' enjoyed fresh food with a hit of borax, formaldehyde, sulfuric acid, saltpeter, or copper sulfate to name a few. Preservatives routinely used by the biggest, most notable food and meat processing companies. The results were hideous. Wiley discovered we were poisoning families with bright green peas soaked in copper sulfate, a pesticide; feeding our babies milk laced with formaldehyde, an embalmer.

"Wiley's attack on the powerful lynchpins and lobbyists hacked-off Teddy Roosevelt and he threatened to bury it. But Upton Sinclair's book, *The Jungle* came out in time to blow the lid off Chicago's slaughterhouses—exposing the filth, corruption, exploitation and disregard for immigrant workers and American families. Wiley's cause was stoked. Roosevelt signed the Pure Food and Drug Act and the Meat Inspection Act on the same day. Unfortunately, the food industry lobbyists were tenacious. They continued to line pockets in D.C. and the Pure Food Act was gutted by the GRAS loophole in 1958. You'd think the battle for safe, healthy food would be a slam dunk. But these gangs of thieves continue to hold the government hostage. Mag, I have no frigging idea what I'm doing. Here's where Bruce enters the picture."

"Wait. Remind me what GRAS means."

"Generally Recognized As Safe—it's a catchall with an epidemic spread. It started with a few hundred additives like salt, pepper, mint. Now it's in the tens of thousands—maybe hundreds of thousands. FDA employees are rewarded by the number of GRAS requests they process and punished with make-work assignments when they challenge an application and productivity drops. After a few months, adaptation kicks in. The approval stamp promises better evaluations, bigger raises, and stress-free days. Who wouldn't?"

"Where does Bruce enter the picture?"

"Mag, what I'm about to tell you is Oz's holy grail—protected from light, the human touch, the spoken word, you name it. Jacques gave us an 'Apostolic Pardon' for tonight's discussion. Once we're done talking about Bruce, that's it. We never mention him again. And you won't talk about him or contact him. Mag, I saw you roll your eyes. I'm not playing this up. In fact, I'm worried there's no way to give it enough weight. If leaked, it'll cost lives. I need you to agree to these terms. If not, I won't say more."

Maggie had been half-in on the conversation about food tampering—but this kicked her adrenalin into overdrive. "Holy crap, Sam. I wasn't ready for the . . . drama. I'm not making light of what you said, I'm knocked off balance."

"I'm glad because I meant it to be critical and dramatic. If I tell you about Bruce's role, you'll carry some dreadful images the rest of your life; images you'll never be free to talk or write about. If I don't tell you, you and Tekla might end up in one of those images.

"In that case, I found my balance. Tell me."

"Bruce is one of those guys that guys love and women lust. His attraction is obvious in his energy, brilliance, and self-confidence. What makes Bruce more compelling? His bi-sexual belligerence and disdain for the ordinary. Women want to seduce him; men want to seduce him or be his wingman. You may not like hearing this take on him, but it's part of Bruce's dossier—hidden with other records Oz kept safe from public view.

"You see, Bruce works both sides. He makes a boatload of money from both Oz and the industries Oz wants to nail. He's a double-agent and both sides know he works both sides. It sounds crazy, but here's why it works. Bruce gives both clients the option of using force without taking on the threat of legal action or adverse public opinion.

"When plans were made to abduct you, me and Tekla, Bruce started the bidding war between the juicers and Oz. Once he had his price from each side, he then negotiated the best outcomes with the least threat to both the juicers and Oz.

"You were easy to track. Once Bruce got the documents you copied, he put you on notice to stay put. Bruce had already negotiated a price with Oz for your abduction. When you tipped Bruce off about the agents in the hotel, he called one of his thugs to call them off, not knock them off. Bruce called it collateral damage. He's well-connected and trusted by the lone-wolves and crime syndicate hitmen. He has a reputation of paying well and being honest about his double-dipping. According to Jacques, the bad guys keep track of the number of jobs they do for Bruce to up their bragging rights. When the bad guys get caught, Bruce defends them. When it looks like he'll lose the case, he calls in his chits and forces the win.

"Jacques says everyone keeps waiting for Bruce to get nailed, but he's like Teflon. Bruce doesn't get caught. Apparently, he doesn't name names, brag about his crimes or conquests, make promises he can't keep, or play favorites. When he needs leverage, he writes his own lore about double-crossers who met fates worthy of lore. Jacques insists Bruce could care less about the dispute or the money. For Bruce, it really is all about the deal.

"Whatever his motivation, he's spectacularly successful and Oz doesn't want anyone else negotiating the dark side of human rights and social justice. I believe you when you say it's over, there's no attraction. We're having this conversation because Bruce will be walking me through the food industry's minefields. And you, my love, are the kryptonite. I can't make this walk if there's any risk you'll rekindle that flame."

Maggie's mind and heart were racing. The best she could hope for was a photo finish. She had to stop . . . stop and look Sam in the eyes and tell him the truth . . . truth that was rumbling in her stomach and cramping her leg muscles. *Now,* she thought, *time to show up.*

Maggie turned toward Sam and saw his confidence, with a hint of worry, maybe fear. "I had no idea you were involved in something this big, intimidating, and scary as hell. My first instinct is to walk back this conversation and ask for the short version. My second instinct is to give you all the assurance you need. Instead, I'm going to take a few deep breaths and be as honest and loving as I can be."

"Maggie, I know."

"You know what?"

"I know you've seen Bruce since we've been back. I heard you wanted to draw the line in the sand. My question is whether that line is deep enough."

"You knew that?"

"I did. And, if your next question is who told me, I can't say."

"All right. That was part of the truth I wanted to cover. Six months after we got back, I met Bruce in his office during work hours. I told him what happened in the past was the past. He's a game-player and he wanted to tease it out. I ended up crying because I was so frustrated and confused. I let him hug me goodbye and he was very . . . hmm . . . insistent. He wanted more. Nothing happened. I left. End of story. I haven't seen him or talked to him since. Although I wish you'd told me when you found out, that ball was clearly in my court. You should have heard it from me."

"Mag, it's okay. My question is whether you've teased it out enough to know where you are."

"I'm not sure. I love you as much as I know how to love. That's what I'd say if I thought love was a verb. But I'm not sure it's a verb. I'm beginning to think love is a noun. We are love. Okay, I just saw you roll your eyes. Stay with me!" Maggie shook her head, then began running her index finger around the curlicued nap of the old chenille bedspread. When she looked up, she saw Sam's worry. "Sam Tervo, I want you to hear me say this. What I want is to live my life with you—you and me—raising Tekla, growing old together. I can't imagine . . . don't want to imagine . . . what life would be like if I didn't have you here, sitting on this bed, talking to me with such openness, tenderness, and trust.

"What scares me was how easily I was pulled away by Bruce's charm and flattery. From the moment I met him, I knew he was a player. Yet, I let him seduce me into thinking he was chasing me on a white steed with a suit of armor. What sane adult woman thinks like that? I'm not stupid.

"So, no, I don't trust myself to say whether I've teased it out enough to know where I am, but I promise I'm far better at finding my way. I'd never do anything to put you or Tekla at risk. You can count on that. As to kindling, Mr. Boxer Shorts, you're my fire. You can take your walk across that minefield. I'll be here. Tekla and I have your back."

Sam held Maggie's face in his hands, looked in her eyes and said, "I'm fine with love as a noun; let's see where it takes us." Slipping out of bed, Sam walked across the room, flicked off the overhead lights, then stood at the open window. The Earth had finally turned its back on the sun and a hoot owl was claiming the night.

END

DETROIT EIGHT SERIES | BOOK THREE

# Afterword

Dear Reader,

I hope you enjoyed *One Wingbeat Away*. If you wouldn't mind, I'd love a quick review on Amazon.

In the following Epilogue, the Y2K Apocalypse looms large. Featuring Tekla and Carter, it opens generational opportunities we've only dreamt about. Still looming and looking for the next wingbeat.

Peace and Love,

# Epilogue

# Y2K Apocalypse

HOUSTON, TEXAS | JANUARY 1, 2000—Tekla felt his shadow before he leaned over and whispered in her ear, "Do not be afraid, Grasshopper. The sun is rising. SUVs are flying up and down Westheimer. And some DJ just hollered, 'Houstonians, time to get your lazy asses outta bed!'"

Peeking over J.W. Marriott's eight-hundred-count cotton sheets, Tekla said, "You sure? No signs of Y2K?"

Bare-chested, a white towel wrapped around his waist, Carter bent over and stalked his way to the window. "Hmm. Doesn't look like the world's crashing in on itself. No visible signs of Armageddon—lights burning; fountains running; no traffic jams. But don't know jack-squat about our bank accounts or credit cards."

"Are we cash poor? Do we need to get to an ATM?"

"The day is young. I say we stake out Tiffany & Company in case their security system fails. By now I bet the looters have snagged all the best spots."

"Carter, you sure didn't fall far from Uncle Clyde's tree when it comes to wicked humor."

"Tekla, do you have any idea how much it still creeps me out when you call my dad uncle?"

"I wouldn't go there. I promise no one's thinking incest when they see us together."

"I see. So, being my cousin is better than being my ho?"

Growling, Tekla threw one of the four goose-down pillows at him.

Carter caught the pillow and tossed it back as he headed to the shower. *Good god,* thought Tekla, *how did I get the ovaries to put moves on my first crush? When Uncle Clyde caught us making out in the basement sixteen years ago, I thought he'd kill Carter. I never expected we'd break his heart.* Tekla closed her eyes; freeing her mind to, once again, recompose her memoir-in-waiting:

> Have I introduced Sam and Maggie, my nerdy parents? They belong to The Detroit Eights—a group of old Freedom Riders stuck in a Kumbaya song. They still see themselves as bad-ass militants, but rock-out when they hear John Denver singing Country Road.
>
> Okay these descriptions are hyperbolic—literary excess so you get the picture in a few words. But there's no way to exaggerate The Eights in my life. They're family. When they met at the Webster house; or when Sam, Clyde and Willie got together in the Webster's backyard to talk trash, I—Tekla Moonwalker Tervo—got to play with the wrecking crew; the three strange, exotic, rowdy Webster boys.
>
> At eleven I was struck dumb with love. Carter Sam Webster was only fourteen and he barely noticed girls his age. For sure he completely missed—or dismissed—my intense, obsessive interest in everything he liked: guitar playing, chess games, stamp collecting and Detroit Tiger baseball. Over the next three years, each time we saw the Websters, I wore my Tiger baseball cap and orange and blue Tiger tee shirt. Then, with my period and training bra, I began to uncover my inner vamp.

I'd eavesdrop on Maggie's conversations with Aunt Blanche hoping I'd hear something about Carter. One day Maggie told Aunt Blanche that I was taking puberty far too seriously and she hoped it would pass. I remember thinking adults were clueless.

During the summer of 1983, my fourteenth year, I began planning how I'd seduce Carter. First, I experimented with my libido. Wearing shorts and a halter top, I tried masturbation—in the weeds, near the ravine, under the sun. In this makeshift laboratory behind our house, surrounded by chickweed, pokeweed, and foxtail, I began to sync with words like hot, erotic, orgasmic—through the heat of the sun, my nakedness, and a few tattered pages of "Fear of Flying."

The tension between the rush of pleasure and risk of being caught blew my mind. More than once I worried these cheap thrills would turn me into a hooker or gangster. Lucky for me, summers are short in Michigan and I grew boobs. I called them headlights because, suddenly, boys at school who never noticed me began acting like startled deer when I walked down the hall.

By the time I turned fifteen, I'd scored more than a few hours of practice making out with real boys—clothes on, French-kissing, some petting, but never going all the way. Carter, eighteen by then, had more than his share of dates, but no real girlfriend until his senior year. In September, Carter would start at Wayne State. According to the Webster House Rules, he'd live at home and ride the bus his first two years before getting a place of his own or bunking with one of his older brothers—both options on his dime. As for me, I was doing cartwheels over news that Carter's girlfriend, Nina, would be one-hundred-forty miles away doing the Electric Slide at Western Michigan U in Kalamazoo!

A few weeks before Carter's freshman orientation, The Eights were meeting in the Webster's dining room. I was in the basement listening to Carter practice his guitar. The stone walls, hard-packed dirt floor and dim lighting gave it a woodsy, campy feel—as if we were alone in a small puptent. In my most melodramatic fifteen-year-old mind, it seemed like I'd been waiting for the perfect time for years and decided it would be then, right there, in the basement.

Before Carter put away his guitar, I asked him to show me how to play a few chords. That was all it took. We were down to underwear on one of the two bare wood and canvas cots from the Army Surplus store. That's when Uncle Clyde walked in and lost it. He lifted Carter by his waist, shoved him across the room, and through gritted teeth seethed, "Put your pants on and wait for me in the backyard." With his head still turned away from me, Uncle Clyde handed me a clean, folded sheet from the top of the dryer and started to sob.

I'd never heard a grown man cry before. I wasn't sure what to do. Although I wanted to cry, it felt wrong, like I was feeling sorry for myself. I listened to each footfall as Clyde followed Carter upstairs. The steps carried disappointment, regret, shame. Shaking, I resisted the instinct to curl up in a fetal position and nurse my fear. Instead, I sat up. When I heard the back door open and close, I leaned forward as if I could hear what was being said. At that moment I knew I wanted to marry a man strong enough to cry—a man like Uncle Clyde, like Carter would be one day.

Barred from talking on the phone or being alone with each other sent our stoked hormones into overdrive. At family gatherings Carter and I used our eyes, faces and body language to speak. And, of course, we met at Wayne State on weekends when Maggie thought I was out with friends. Or so I thought she thought. Turns out Maggie was much less concerned. Always the poet, Maggie later confessed she referred to our basement scene as 'Shakespeare in Detroit.'

"Woman, are you still horizontal? Shower's yours, so catch some hot water before we lose power. I'll grab a copy of the *Chronicle* and meet you downstairs for breakfast."

"Seriously? You're leaving me here, alone? What if the automatic locks don't work and I get caught in this hermetically-sealed room without air, water, food? Oh god, you can't do this to me. I could end up being the first person to die in Y2K!"

"Unless you're inviting me for a roll in the sack, I'm heading south, probably taking the stairs."

"Okay, but when you get to the street level, I want you to walk outside and look up at our room. If I'm flattened against the plate glass, pounding my fists on the windows, and crying your name, like Dustin Hoffman did in *The Graduate*, will you please, please come rescue me?"

"No shit? Dustin Hoffman was crying my name?" Carter laughed as he ducked the *Houston* magazine Tekla threw his way, then slipped out the door.

Stretching out on the bed, a smile crossed Tekla's face and infected every cell in her body. God knows they'd worked hard. Y2K meant dooms-day sale prices on hotels, conference centers, air travel and catering fees. Their Continental flight from Detroit last night held less than twenty passengers. When they arrived at Houston's Intercontinental Airport at eight, someone could have shot a hockey puck down the concourse without hitting anyone. The city was idling—gas-filled cars parked in driveways, not garages; gallon jugs of fresh water on kitchen counters; flashlights and spare batteries on lamp tables; and first-aid kits, cash, coin, three changes of clothes, and ninety days of medication in grab-and-go bags by the front door. Inside the 610 Loop, streets and highways were eerily dark and quiet. The chichi Galleria Area around the J. W. Marriott looked like an abandoned movie set.

Tekla knew most of the country would be hunkered down in front of TVs on New Year's Day, watching football, and hoping the electrical power grid wouldn't shut down during a Hail Mary pass. For Carter and her, it would be a long, emotion-packed day—one that promised to flip the balance of power and transform lives.

Sam and Uncle Clyde's dream of community-based organic food producers and sellers—with negotiated nutritional and health metrics—was flourishing in fourteen countries. With almost two million people and six-hundred-sixty-five square miles of mixed zoning, Houston would be the largest, least agrarian, least fertile metroplex to explore a partnership with Oz. Houston had pulled together the heavy hitters in state, county, and city government. Bruce, Sam's lifelong partner and constant nemesis, was bringing in the oppositional side—food and beverage manufacturers, trucking companies, unions, and politicians threatened by any whiff of socialism. By now, they knew these Food Pods worked.

Closing her eyes, Tekla planned to take these last few empty minutes to steep in the unhurried, liminal sensation between now and then. As Maggie liked to say, our future is one wingbeat away.

# Acknowledgements

It wasn't a diabolical plot. When I first invited Sandra Whitener, Kirsten McLean, Frank Cooley, and Dianne Wesselhoft to serve as my *Illustrious but Unpaid Editorial Staff*, we all thought we were onboard to write/edit one novel. No one knew it would morph into a series. None of us signed up for five years of living with The Eights. Helping me through untold numbers of revisions—rewriting, retitling, restarting—we talked about the characters as if they were real, and they became real. This series was developed and held together by their intelligence, warmth, and grace.

To friends and relatives who cheered me on, served as beta readers, muses—or met me at Las Palomas to stir the embers over chips and salsa—my deepest affection and gratitude. A special shoutout to Scott Wiggerman and David Meischen in Albuquerque—good friends, poets, writers, artists—who gave birth to an incredible collection of exercises and advice by well-known poets in *Wingbeats: Exercises & Practice in Poetry*. They waved away my concern for appropriating the word wingbeat.

Once again, I had the remarkable good fortune to work with Danielle Hartman Acee, copy/content editing, interior design, social media consulting, publicity. We've 'grown up' together, become friends. New to the team is Tim Barber of Dissect Designs in England. After a few energetic exchanges and several pandemic delays, Tim almost telepathically created Wingbeat's extraordinary cover. Both calm, seasoned veterans, they were seamless in navigating the technical, emotional, intellectual, and artistic pathways to transform the manuscript into a book.

To be sure, The Detroit Eight Series could not have been written without the love and coaching of life mentors who taught me about grace, acceptance, equality, oneness, and otherness. Black, white, multi-racial friends and relatives, who had the audacity to speak their truth, breathe life into my characters, and help me find my voice.

Then there's this behind-the-scenes man I live with, Loren. On-call editor, hugger, dog walker, hunter-gatherer, poet, psychotherapist, humorist, looks past the third-day-pajamas-and-crumbs-to-tell-me-I'm-beautiful kind of guy. During the endless days of the pandemic, we were inspired by the human spirit and assaulted by the corruption, brutality, and racism in a country we thought we knew. Loren tempted me with poetry; I revived my radical activist bard. Relationship surviving, poems Zooming, world still demanding love and attention.

# About the Author

Born in Detroit, Kathleen Hall coauthored the award-winning non-fiction *The Otherness Factor,* before launching into historical fiction with The Detroit Eight in *If the Moon Had Willow Trees* and *Livonia |The Whitest City.*

A writer, poet, lawyer, mediator, and workplace investigator, Kathleen's lifelong activism has been devoted to championing equal rights and promoting the power of diversity. She lives in Austin, Texas with her partner, Loren, Emma Dog, herds of deer roaming the streets, red foxes sunbathing in their miniature backyard, and armadillos tottering across the driveway.

www.ingramcontent.com/pod-product-compliance
Lightning Source LLC
LaVergne TN
LVHW091148080826
845145LV00008B/2292

* 9 7 8 0 9 9 0 3 9 0 4 7 3 *